P9-DDU-296

PRAISE FOR
THE GREAT JEFF

"Jeff's search to understand himself and the harsh world around him is breathtaking." —Patricia Reilly Giff, author of Newbery Honor winners *Pictures of Hollis Woods* and *Lily's Crossing*

"In a body of stellar work, *The Great Jeff* may be Abbott's finest." —Nora Raleigh Baskin, award-winning author of *Anything But Typical*, *Ruby on the Outside*, and *Nine, Ten: A September 11 Story*

★ "An exquisitely moving yet completely age-appropriate dive into a kid's experience of impoverishment." —*The Bulletin*, starred review

"A moving, realistic coming-of-age tale." —*Kirkus Reviews*

"A hopeful coming-of-age story that portrays the challenges of poverty in a realistic and relatable way." —*Booklist*

"A powerful and realistic story of a boy coming of age with a family in crisis." —*School Library Journal*

"For fans of *Firegirl*, this follow-up is a must-read.... This novel is a solid addition to any library." —*School Library Connection*

THE
GREAT
JEFF

32140004488462

THE
GREAT
JEFF

TONY ABBOTT

Little, Brown and Company
New York Boston

JUN 2 2 2020

This book is a work of fiction. Names, characters, places, and incidents are the product of the author's imagination or are used fictitiously. Any resemblance to actual events, locales, or persons, living or dead, is coincidental.

Copyright © 2019 by Tony Abbott
Discussion Guide copyright © 2020 by Tony Abbott
Excerpt from *Firegirl* copyright © 2006 by Tony Abbott

Cover art copyright © 2019 by Mina Price. Cover design by Nicole Brown.
Cover copyright © 2019 by Hachette Book Group, Inc.

Hachette Book Group supports the right to free expression and the value of copyright. The purpose of copyright is to encourage writers and artists to produce the creative works that enrich our culture.

The scanning, uploading, and distribution of this book without permission is a theft of the author's intellectual property. If you would like permission to use material from the book (other than for review purposes), please contact permissions@hbgusa.com. Thank you for your support of the author's rights.

Little, Brown and Company
Hachette Book Group
1290 Avenue of the Americas, New York, NY 10104
Visit us at LBYR.com

Originally published in hardcover and ebook by Little, Brown and Company in March 2019
First Trade Paperback Edition: March 2020

Little, Brown and Company is a division of Hachette Book Group, Inc.
The Little, Brown name and logo are trademarks of Hachette Book Group, Inc.

The publisher is not responsible for websites (or their content) that are not owned by the publisher.

Excerpts on pages 77, 119, 129, and 132 from THE HOUSE ON MANGO STREET. Copyright © 1984 by Sandra Cisneros. Published by Vintage Books, an imprint of Random House, Inc., and in hardcover by Alfred A. Knopf in 1994. By permission of Susan Bergholz Literary Services, New York, NY and Lamy, NM. All rights reserved.

The Library of Congress has cataloged the hardcover edition as follows:
Names: Abbott, Tony, 1952– author.
Title: The great Jeff / by Tony Abbott.
Description: First edition. | New York ; Boston : Little, Brown and Company, 2019. |
Summary: Thirteen-year-old Jeff's life spirals downward into homelessness after his alcoholic mother loses her job.
Identifiers: LCCN 2018020156| ISBN 9780316479691 (hardcover) | ISBN 9780316479707 (ebook) | ISBN 9780316479677 (library edition ebook)
Subjects: | CYAC: Homeless persons—Fiction. | Single-parent families—Fiction. | Poverty—Fiction. | Middle schools—Fiction. | Schools—Fiction.
Classification: LCC PZ7.A1587 Gr 2019 | DDC [Fic]—dc23
LC record available at https://lccn.loc.gov/2018020156

ISBNs: 978-0-316-47971-4 (pbk.), 978-0-316-47970-7 (ebook)

Printed in the United States of America

LSC-C

10 9 8 7 6 5 4 3 2 1

To young people
and their families

CHAPTER 1
ME

I was five when I saw my first person die.

My grandfather worked for the railroad. He was a conductor until he lost half of one of his legs to diabetes two years after I was born. That's a sugar disease that kills your circulation. Your nerves die because your blood doesn't get all the way to the things farthest away from your heart. Your feet and legs.

Grandpa seemed old to me then. I realized later he wasn't really. Sixty-seven. Not old enough to just die. But he looked ancient, gray and white, not much of him there.

It was my fifth birthday. I was standing in the doorway of his room. Grandpa had lived with us for a few years but hadn't come with us when we went away that weekend. He didn't really go anywhere. We came home and found him gurgling in his throat. *Jeff,* my mother called from the kitchen. *Jeff, don't bother him.* She was phoning 911 and his doctor, whose name was written next to the wall phone. My father was around somewhere, but I don't remember where.

My grandmother had passed away from heart problems before I was born, so Grandpa was alone. Mom took care of him and loved him more than anyone. He had a funny smell that day. His breathing was wet and crackly. Grandpa loved me a lot, I think he did. When his eyelids fluttered and opened, I went over to his bed. It was in the corner of the little downstairs room between two gray walls. He smelled like pee. *Where is his caretaker! Jeff, get back in here.* I looked down the sheet covering him to see if I could find pee stains. His regular leg looked like a bone resting on the pillow under the sheet, that's how skinny it was. One white foot stuck out. It was black on the bottom of the toes and on his heel. The other leg ended above where his knee would be.

When I looked at his face his eyes were on me.

"Jeffie," he said.

My mom was calling *Jeff, Jeff,* but the louder she got the less I heard her. He said some wet things for a while and he sounded choky. I answered when I thought it was a question. His breath was thick and bad, and not all he was saying made sense to me.

When he told me the thing that was going to be the last thing he said, I didn't know it yet, so I tried to answer him. While I was talking he coughed funny and his mouth stayed open and he was dead. I was the only one in his room for that. After a minute or two of looking at him I touched his cheek. His skin was warm even a little after he died.

I remembered Grandpa this afternoon when my mom came home from work and was calling "Jeff! Jeff!" from the second she opened the door.

Don't ask me why I thought about an old man lying in his bed between two gray walls, but I did.

"In the basement," I yelled.

"Get up here."

Normally Rich Downing is over on Fridays and we read comic books together or watch TV in my basement. Other days he has things to do and doesn't come. Sometimes I go to his house, but it's weird there.

When I came up the stairs to the kitchen she whispered, "Is your friend Tom here?"

"No, Mom," I said, "it's Rich now. It's never Tom anymore. He's not my friend. Rich is. Rich has come over every Friday for a long time now." I tried to tell her that he was actually in the bathroom right now, but she cut me off.

"Well, I'm on vacation!" She slammed her bag on the kitchen table, spilling stuff out of it. Her eyes were wet and red. That wasn't new. The new part was that they were bloodshot right after work instead of the morning after being out with her nurse friends.

I think I laughed somehow. "Vacation? Disney World, obviously. I'll go pack—"

"They fired me."

"What?"

"Fairchild cut two nursing positions. And when the fat one made a stink, saying they fired her because she was fat, they turned right around and gave her my job. Jeff, I don't have a job."

My blood froze. "So what does that mean? When are you getting it back?"

"Ha." She opened the refrigerator and pulled out a tall green bottle. "You don't get it back, smarty. And because I've only been there since July, less than three months, I won't get unemployment benefits either. Honey, we're up the creek."

Which is not what she really said.

"What about St. Damien's?" I asked.

She drank her glass empty and refilled it. "What *about* it?"

St. Damien's is the Catholic high school you go to after St. Catherine's, which I had to leave after seventh grade because of no money. Rich still went to St. Catherine's. Everybody I knew still went there and was planning to go to Damien's next fall. Some of the teachers were moving up, too.

She looked at me. "Well?"

If you really want to know, my father ripped something out of me when he stopped paying for Catholic school, and I had to go to public school with only a year left. That's a curse. I'd built up a thing at St. Catherine's. A style. Not everybody liked it, but everybody knew it.

If you know me, you won't think I can love anything and you'd be wrong. St. Catherine's had a smell I smelled every morning when I walked inside from the bus. That smell said that no matter what I'd left at home, I was going to be all right there. Not that I ever asked for it either, but Mrs. Tracy always cut me some slack when I said something off-the-wall. Not all the teachers did but she did. Hard to build up an adoring fan base at a new school, floating around with nine hundred other kids.

I stared at her face through the bottom of her wineglass. "Dad said after this one stinking year, he'd send more money. You said you were saving, too, and together it would be enough so I could go to Damien's next year."

"Saving? When did I say that?"

"In the summer. 'Because it means so much to you,' you said. I hate public school, Mom, I *hate* it."

"Well, you're going to have to hate it a little longer."

"But all my friends—"

"Friends?" Her face pruned up. "Jeff, your *friends* abandoned you. They let you go like you were nothing. Real friends don't do that. Ha, but *your* friends did. Some friends, I say."

It was true, I guess. Some of them abandoned me. One of them mostly.

"Not Mrs. Tracy. Not Rich either," I said. "Who by the way is—"

"And your father? Well, he was plain lying to you. He lies to everybody. Sometimes I think that's where you learned it. Listening to him."

"Thanks a lot, Mom."

She made a noise in her throat and lowered her glass. "I'm sorry, that wasn't fair, but come on. Your father doesn't have two shiny dimes to rub together." Which she said as if it made her happy. "But I'll tell you what. He'd better pay up now. He'd better chip in, and not for school, that's all I have to say." She poured out a third glass. "We'll catch up on our rent."

"Rent, what rent? I thought we owned our house."

"If you think that, you don't pay enough attention."

"You never said we didn't own it. People own houses."

"We never owned it, honeybunch. And I'm a little late on last month's rent. Except, you know what, I'll get it from your father now...."

She didn't finish but started buzzing around the kitchen, turning over stuff as if she couldn't find her cell phone, which had slid out of her bag onto the table. She fluttered all over, muttering, because she didn't want me saying anything else. I knew the way she did things. The room belonged to her now, and I was just standing in it.

—

My father hasn't lived with us for almost four years. He's a paper dad, if you know what I mean. If there was a test and the question was, *Who is your father?* I would have to put his name down: James R. Hicks. But he was gone long before he left the house. He hated when Grandpa came to live with us. He wanted to hide him away, give him the closed-in back porch instead of a regular room.

"He's always here!" he'd say when he came home from being out.

"Because he can't walk!" my mother would answer, which I'm sure Grandpa heard.

Then my father "fell in love" (which I don't really know what that means) and Mom found out and he moved out of the house. For a little while he was living in Stamford, which is a few towns down, and I used to see him fairly regularly. Then he moved to New York with his girlfriend, and I don't see him as much, only on holidays, a few times a year.

He paid Mom some, because when your dad bolts it doesn't matter why or what he says, he still has to pay for the kids he had with your mother. More paper, right? Public school was free and St. Catherine's wasn't, so when money got tight, like Mom said it did this past summer, they bounced me down to public school for the year.

With her cell phone tucked between her ear and her shoulder, Mom clanked among the bottles on the shelf in the fridge, keeping the door open with her knee. "Is that it? Where's the other one?"

Did she think I drank it?

There were guys after my father left. I heard names, that's all. Carl. Paul, who she called Skip. She talked about Ron for a few months, but he faded away, too, or moved. She never brought them home, I don't want you to think that. How gross would it be, my mom with a boyfriend? But I never saw them. Maybe she just didn't want them to meet me. Bottom line, none of them lasted very long.

She let the fridge door close and slammed her phone on the tabletop, swearing a streak at my father. "Voice mail, my foot!"

She grabbed her glass again, when the toilet suddenly flushed and Rich was there and we both stared at Mom sucking red drops from her empty glass.

"Who in heaven's name are you?" she screamed.

Rich stared at me while the color drained from his face. "Uh..."

"Good one, Mom. Terrify the guests, why don't you. Come on, Rich." I pulled him back down to the basement while she leaned against the counter and called after me in a sloppy voice. *Jeff, Jeff.* I knew she'd soon be crying. She always cries after wine.

"Well, that was nice," I said to Rich when we got downstairs. "But that's"—and here I jerked my arms out like a stand-up comedian—"*Mommy!*"

He laughed, so I kept this evil grin on and wiggled my eyebrows and did a silly walk to keep him laughing, which he did, but he didn't know who I was doing.

"I get it," he finally said. "My dad explodes sometimes. Maybe I should go."

"Nah. It doesn't matter."

Rich went home anyway, closing the door behind him while my mom whimpered on the living room couch.

———

Funny, when I think about the last person to really love me, and the first person to have so much trouble with it, I see my mother running into my grandfather's room that day he died. She swatted my hand away from his face as if I'd done something horrible, started bawling like she was now, and kissed his wrinkled dead cheek over and over, saying, "Daddy, oh, Daddy."

CHAPTER 2
DUCK SOUP

So you've probably guessed this isn't going to be a laugh riot.

On the other hand, I should tell you how funny I am. How I go around basically happy. I had this friend for a few years who I already mentioned, Tom Bender. I cracked him up every time. Just saying his name now makes me want to spit, but I could make him choke on his tongue with what I came up with. Smart stuff, too. I'm quick in my head and it goes right to my mouth. Hilarious.

Most people at my new school don't get my kind of funny. I mean, they do, a little. Like Colin and Josh, but they're only in two of my classes. And I've been there only a few weeks, so no one's had the full Jeff experience.

I'm like the kid who has to touch stuff in stores when he passes down the aisle. I see things and have to respond. It's how I flow. Some people think what I say is mean. Or that I try to hurt them or that I don't care if I do.

Some of what I say or do might sting, but I don't always mean it to. I just see things going on and make a crack. Like Groucho Marx. I still remember when I was nine and saw the Marx Brothers movie called *Duck Soup*. Tom Bender was there for that. It's a crazy story about a fake country going to war. I couldn't catch my breath and my throat and chest hurt I laughed so hard. Groucho does this silly crouching walk and twitches his eyebrows and gets a lot of dirty looks, like I do. Tom said I was like him, but without the mustache. Sorry. I won't talk about Tom again.

Not that any of that matters. When people make up their minds about you, they only see you one way, which is the easy way for them. What I'm trying to say is that mostly when I wake up, I have a smile on my face. Sometimes I laugh myself right out of bed. It's only later, when I remember, that my stomach begins to hurt.

———

Mom finally caught up with Dad on the phone late that night. I don't know what he said, but they arranged that we'd go visit him in New York the following week.

"Once we get to his *apartment*," she said at breakfast on Saturday, as if his place were all chandeliers and fireplaces, "I'll tell him exactly what happened with my job, and what a stew we're in, then we'll have a talk."

"I have things to say, too. Plus, his place is tiny."

"And there's something you need to know," she said,

lowering her voice and pressing my arm with her fingers. "Until then, until we see your father, you're not saying anything to anybody. Not a word about me losing my job. Not a single word."

"What would I say?" I asked her. "To who?"

"Because as far as they're concerned, everything's normal. No one can know. You're not telling Tom or any of your other friends, you hear me?"

"I don't have anybody to tell. And I told you a thousand times, I'm not friends with Tom Bender anymore. I hate this. You never listen when I talk."

"Don't smart-mouth me."

He hasn't been my friend since before I left St. Catherine's. First of all, I took pity on him. He was chubby and klutzy, but he was usually around and thought I was funny, which he was right about. Then, all of a sudden, he became a jerk over this girl. Forgetting all the junk we did together, he started telling bad stories about me and my mom, I'm sure he did. Sorry, that's it. No more stupid Tom Bender.

"What difference does it make if people know about your job anyway?" I asked.

Mom had moved to another room and didn't hear. I finished my eggs alone and rinsed the plate. Dried egg yolk is hard to get off.

Then she was back, flapping a stack of envelopes in her hand. "Here's something else you need to know. Don't be

12

surprised if I cut down on things. These bills are eating us alive. And I don't care what they say, first thing Monday I'm going to the unemployment office and register."

She winked as if we were getting back at someone in a sneaky way.

"I thought you couldn't," I said. "That they wouldn't give you anything—"

"Let them tell me to my face when I'm standing in front of them with a stack of bills I can't pay. If I look them square in the eye we'll get benefits. It's insurance. They'll have to give me it. Until I find a new thing."

She was so scattered and scared it was hard to make out what she meant. One thing was clear: If I got lying from my father, I'm pretty sure I got the victim thing from her.

"You mean they pay you not to work? They should. You've worked forever."

"You bet I have," she said. "I'm taking care of it. I'm on top of it."

She ought to be. She did the same thing when the hospital let her go in January for being late too many times. I should have seen that coming. Even last fall, a year ago, a few times when I came home from school she'd be there, sleeping. It took her until this summer to find another job. Now after less than three months she'd lost that one, too.

"Plus, you need to wash that hair," she said, sitting

down at the table across from where I'd been. "People'll think our water's turned off. Well, not yet. So get in there. I'll make a grocery list. You want a comic if I see one at the store?"

"I have all the new ones."

"Good. We'll save four dollars."

———

So, yeah, I took a shower. After I toweled off I dressed in the same jeans but a clean shirt, my usual procedure. I wondered what it actually meant that Mom had lost her job. How long would it be before she had another one? Could I believe that she was taking care of it? Should I do anything differently?

I came downstairs to find she'd left for the store.

It was after ten so I headed to Rich Downing's house.

CHAPTER 3
BEST FRIENDS

It's not like I chose Rich for a friend.

He chose me because I make him laugh. Hard not to do. We're on different levels and I'm so much quicker it isn't funny, except, of course, it is. He mostly comes to my house because I have better comics and we're usually alone there. It was too soon to figure out if Mom's no-job would change things like that.

Four short blocks and a dogleg through some back-yards is how you get to his place. I wore a jacket and a sweatshirt under. It was cold, but not as cold as last fall, not yet. It was freezing last year at Halloween and we had snow at Thanksgiving.

Only one of their two cars was in the driveway. Rich's father coaches soccer Saturday mornings—Rich's younger sister plays—but his mother is usually home, and he has an older sister, too, so I can't just walk in. I rang the bell.

His mother smiled when she opened the front door. The smile was the right shape and all, except her eyes looked over my shoulder at passing cars or the future or somewhere. I mumbled, "Hello, Mrs. Downing," like you're supposed to. "Is Rich home?" Which she didn't even have to answer because he came bounding down the stairs to let me in, while she went off to another room. We went into what he called the den.

"I have to play you this. I just learned it." He picked up his electric guitar and switched on the amplifier. The amp snapped loudly and a red light glowed on the dashboard.

He got the guitar over the summer. His father had been teaching him for a while, but this was Rich's first electric. "Ready?" He hunched over it and placed the fingers of his left hand one by one on the strings. I could tell it was a song he had just learned because that's not how you play anything good. To really play, your fingers move where they need to without thinking. I didn't know how to play, but Rich wasn't much better.

He has two electric guitars. Well, one of them's his dad's, a big old gold thing covered with chrome and gold knobs. If it's there, I mostly just jang the open strings and fool with the knobs to make cool effects while Rich plays real chords on his. But when both of us play, with his real janging and my fake janging, it almost sounds like a song.

I could learn a musical instrument if I had a chance.

I'm always humming. We used to have a piano at home that my mom played, and my dad bought a drum set once. They got rid of those when Grandpa moved in.

Rich's new song was only four chords, but when he got going it was pretty good. He told me where to press strings on my guitar, so I joined in. We were strumming away and I was thinking he could maybe teach me real chords—because how hard can it be?—when something changed.

I must inspire people to be gross. I don't know. Maybe I ask for it. The Marx Brothers were dirty sometimes. Not really, because their movies are old. But since I'm quick, people think I'm bad even though sometimes I'm just pondering nachos or hang gliding or what the president said about Korea, when all of a sudden *bam*, it happens.

"Courtney must have been wearing last year's sweater," Rich said between chords, leering like an old bum on the street. "It was *tight*."

It's like they think I'm always working dirty stuff over in my mind, so it's okay to be disgusting in front of me in a way you wouldn't be with other people.

I wasn't into it, so I just nodded, but maybe I grinned, too, because then he did.

"Yeah," he said. "You know it!"

Courtney Zisky was this long-haired dark-haired girl in our class at St. Catherine's. I'd say she was hot except she was always pretty cold to me. Which is a small example of my humor. Seriously, Courtney was just really good-looking from every angle, and I liked to look at her, but not everything I thought was creepy.

Just then, Rich's older sister came into the room and together he and I blasted our guitars like a band, and she said something. She had blond hair and was in high school. I don't know why, but I jumped to my feet, mashed up my face like a rock star in pain, and started flailing away on the strings, when she suddenly reaches out and grabs the neck of the guitar.

"Did you hear me, Rich's friend?" Her face was squinched up worse than mine.

I stopped. "What?"

"I said you better not scratch my dad's guitar."

"Yeah. Sure. Don't get all..."

"Don't get all *what*, Rich's friend?" She stood a good half foot taller than me.

I didn't want to tangle. "Don't get all *worried*," I said, and put the guitar gently back on its stand.

Rich had kept playing through this and twisted his fingers into the next chord, but the thing was blown now, ruined. His sister left the room, saying, "I don't like you, Rich's friend."

I gave her a face behind her back. "Let's do something else."

"Yeah, my fingers hurt."

We went out the kitchen door to his backyard. It had

clouded over, and it was colder than before. I picked up a dog ball. Rich's dog died a couple of weeks ago, but her toys were still around. I lobbed it to him.

"Richie, don't go anywhere," his mother called from the back door.

He waved to her and turned to me. "So what your mother was saying yesterday, that's not true, is it? That she got fired and you're going to lose your house? How does that even happen?"

My chest buzzed with adrenaline. "Lose our house? What are you talking about?"

"I thought she said—"

I was so quick I almost didn't know where it came from. "Ha, no! She was joking about somebody at her work. She was doing a voice, that's all. There are all kinds of nutty people at her job. Old freaky ladies."

Rich grinned. "My dad does that a lot. He's great at voices."

My mother had told me not to tell anyone. Maybe it was already too late.

"Rich, lunch," his older sister called, leaning out on the back step. "Just you."

Rich did his best to laugh that off. "She's joking. Come on in."

It wasn't like I *wanted* to be there. I could shut myself in my room or hide out in my basement, but if Mom was back from the store she'd ask me to eat lunch with her or listen to her talk. Since yesterday she seemed weirdly clingy.

"I gotta go anyway," I said. "My mom promised to get me all the new comics."

"Yeah, Mrs. Tracy gave us a ton of reading I really gotta start."

So I left. On the way down the street I sort of realized that Rich was the only actual person in my world, and I didn't even like him that much. How do you like somebody? Would I know if I did?

I stuck my key in the lock and pushed into the house. "Mom?" She was still at the store. The living room seemed farther away than when I left, like I was looking through the wrong end of a telescope. I stood in Grandpa's old room. Maybe I held my breath. I don't know. Lose our house? Friends? St. Catherine's. Rich. Tom Stupid Bender? I felt light-headed and went upstairs, fell into bed, and pulled the covers over my face.

CHAPTER 4
A CHURCH THING

Bad things happen on Fridays. The other days of the week, sure, but Fridays more.

This was, I don't know, October last year? Yeah. October. The Friday before Columbus Day. The misery started even before the morning bus. I had just finished a glass of juice, cranberry, if you want to know, and poured my cereal, when Mom suddenly started screaming and throwing things in Grandpa's old room.

"How could you do this to us?" she cried. "To *me*!"

I ran in to find her swearing at a stack of papers in her hands. The dresser drawers were tipped out, papers, envelopes, cards, photos splayed on the floor.

"What are you doing? Mom?"

"His second life insurance policy! He cashed it in before he died! Why?"

I knelt down and collected the photos. "I don't know what that means."

"It means your father reminded me after all this time that Grandpa had a second life insurance policy and there could be money we forgot to claim when he died, but there isn't. It's worthless!" She threw the papers at the floor and kicked them. Some shiny little cards fluttered out of the mess. She sank to her knees and picked one up.

"Oh! His holy card. From his funeral. Daddy, why..."

The whole thing was insane. Out of nowhere she goes into a meltdown. I sat down next to her, picked up a card, and smelled wine. "You're working a shift today, aren't you?"

She got to her feet. "Later. Never mind. I think I hear your bus."

I stood up. "Will you be here when I get home?"

"Yes. No. I have to work all weekend because everyone else put in their hours first. Your father will take you until Monday."

Take me. Like I was a dog. "I hate it at his place."

"Yeah, well, we all hate something."

It was just as stupid at school that day, too.

Jessica Feeney was a girl in our class who'd been burned in a big fire that made her really hard to look at. People started saying her sister died in the fire, so she got mad and went home, and they all buzzed about that, but my head was all Mom screaming and her wine breath and Grandpa's old dead head and his room torn apart, and I needed something regular or I would explode.

Tom had promised to come over after school like normal, so when we were packing up for dismissal I went over to him. "You're coming, right?"

He didn't really look at me, like Rich's mother doesn't look at me. "I can't," he said. "I have a church thing to do. My mom's making me. She signed me up. To help."

Which didn't sound right. "I thought you were coming over. You said you were going to."

He shrugged. "Yeah, sorry."

"That stinks," I grumbled. "But I'll be home if you want to come after."

Then I heard Mrs. Tracy call him over. I hear her ask something like, "Are you doing anything?" and he shakes his head. Two minutes later, he's digging in Jessica's desk for stuff and I figure Mrs. Tracy asked him to bring Jessica something because he had no plans that afternoon.

So. There wasn't any church thing. He just lied to me. I went over to him. "Church thing, huh?"

He stared at me. "Mrs. Tracy asked me—"

I didn't stay to hear more of his lies. I stumbled out of school to our bus. I didn't say anything to anyone. At my stop, I jumped off and ran home. I threw my backpack on the floor, no, *at* the floor. What just happened? Did I even know? Was I wrong? Did he lie? Maybe he was going to church after all, and I'd gotten it wrong. I went back out, stole across some yards to see what he did.

Yeah. I watched him.

My head was shrieking inside and, hiding behind a tree, I watched him. He walked over to a house. There was a minivan outside. I'd seen it in the school lot. It was her house. He was in there until suppertime. So it was true. He lied to me. He just lied.

I punched the tree trunk over and over.

———

That was the first time I felt I could lose a thing just because of who I was.

I was me, and I wasn't good enough to keep a promise to. Tom Bender had promised to come over but he didn't. You think that wouldn't hurt because I don't care about anything? Wrong again. Maybe I didn't show it right away and tried to block it out, but you can't block out something like that. It's there and it stays there. He lied to me. To my face.

Mom's right. That's what friends do.

CHAPTER 5
THE DAYS OF THE WEEK

First thing Monday Mom asked me to go with her to register for unemployment. I guess she wanted me there to show them she really needed help.

"Should I look hungry?" I said. "Wear crummy clothes, shoes with holes in them? I can do that. Plus, I'll miss school!"

"Nice try. I'm dropping you off right after. You'll miss one class."

"Aww, Mom. All the other kids get to."

"Uh-huh. Just untuck that shirt and practice your cough, mister!"

We so funny, her and me.

At seven thirty on the dot, we rolled up to a place called, if you can believe it, the Great American Job Center. It's the center where you get jobs. In America. Which is great.

She clicked off the Camry, the engine misfired once,

and we got out, shutting our doors at the exact same time. I get that it's weird to do so much with your mother, but it's been just the two of us for years now, and if I didn't have anybody, neither did she.

The office wasn't big, was overheated, and was already packed. When Mom got her number, seventeen away from being called, she got really quiet and dark, like she'd just figured something out. I didn't want to know, so I went outside and walked up and down the street to try to cool off and calm down. It was colder than yesterday, and I wondered what kind of winter it would be. A line started building on the sidewalk outside the door so I went back in. She was only eight numbers away now.

Some kids might think to ask: *Mom, why do you keep losing jobs?* I guess the question didn't occur to me. We just kept rolling along. Losing jobs is a way of life for some people. My dad was the king of losing jobs. He and my mother probably met in an office like this, bumping against each other as they shuffled up to the counter.

"How long you been out of work, pretty?" he would have said.

"Three weeks. You?"

"Eight months. Wanna get a drink?"

She would have laughed. "Before noon? No, sir! I want to keep my place in line. Don't you?"

He'd have shrugged. "What's eight months and a day, sweetie?"

Dad has always had a face like an actor. From the photos I've seen of their wedding, Mom was good-looking, too. But that was fifteen years ago, and you've seen pictures of smokers. All dry skin and face wrinkles. Her cheeks have hollowed out a little, the whites of her eyes faded into yellow—wait, it wasn't *fifteen* years ago, it was barely *fourteen* years ago. I was born so soon after the wedding I could have been in it. Maybe I was.

She got called up, and I sat outside the little cubicle she went into. A mistake. I overheard it come out that she'd been cut to part-time back at her old hospital job four months before they let her go in January, which explained why I sometimes found her home after school. Plus Fairchild Manor, where she'd just been laid off, had reported she'd been late back from lunch three times in the last month, and once didn't come back at all. "It was an emergency," she said to the guy in the cubicle. "I called them right up. It was my car. I called them and told them it wouldn't start."

"It says here they suggested you take a cab, but you didn't want to?"

"A cab! Why not a limo?"

It was nearly third period by the time we finished at the office and were back outside.

"I didn't like that guy," I said. "He was mean to you."

"They all are. I tried to explain, but they don't listen...."

She admitted that Fairchild had offered her another job before she was let go last Friday, and that because she had refused it, she probably wouldn't get unemployment benefits soon, if at all.

"Jeff, the job they offered me was so insulting. They wanted to humiliate me."

"You're too good for that," I said. "*We're* too good for that."

"You bet we are."

She started the car and we drove away and I asked her again to let me skip school.

"Sure, I'll call them," she said. "I'll hear from these guys in five to seven days."

"Can we last that long?"

"Sure, sure," she said again. "I'm already rationing, thinking of ways."

She went quiet and stayed quiet the rest of the way home, busy thinking of more ways while I wondered what we were too good for.

———

On Tuesday, Mr. Maroni, the language arts teacher, was finishing one unit and starting another. Mr. M, which he lets people call him, has a beard and a ponytail and wears button-down shirts and skinny ties under the same old rumply jacket. He never stands still because I don't think he can. He walks up and down and across the room and between the desks, talking the whole time in a stream of words.

Once I stuck my foot way out in the aisle when he came near me, then pulled it back noisily at the last second as a joke. I think he laughed.

Colin Anderson thought it was brilliant. Of course he was right.

Today, Mr. Maroni was strolling across the back of the room when he spun on his heels like a ballerina and waited for us to get settled.

"Okay. Final thoughts on the final book in our poetry unit. Although some people might say our next book is quite poetic, too. Never mind that for now—speak. Speak, and I shall listen! And grade you! Possibly. Anyone?"

Anyone but me.

I don't talk much. About books anyway.

This one was *Out of the Dust*, which is a poetry book that I liked except for all the poems. That's only partly a joke. The book was also supposed to be a story, but you had to connect the poems into a complete story yourself. Fine for some people, but the author made me work for it.

So, of course, joke of jokes, Mr. Maroni calls on me.

"Jeff, any thoughts?"

"Uh...normally, no," I said.

Colin laughed from across the room; so did Josh, who was sitting next to me.

"Uh-huh. Anything you liked about the book?"

"The short lines," I said.

"And yet," he said, standing weirdly still and not taking his eyes off me.

I wondered if this was a chance to give the class the full Jeff treatment, my first in this room. I decided to take it. "Well," I said, "there's the fact that Billie Jo's had a terrible accident. And it kind of sears her, you know? Plus, her mother is gone, which her father can't talk about. And the one thing that might make her feel better—playing the piano—is impossible with her wounded hands...."

"Jeff, don't—"

"To make matters worse," I said, "dust storms are devastating the family farm—"

"Jeff. Really. Thank you for reading the back cover to us."

Someone did applaud me and I got some good laughs, but a pretty girl in the front threw me a really sour look, so I switched gears. Putting the book down, I said, "Seriously, I did learn about droughts and dust storms and farming—"

"Uh-huh. Maybe you should see me after class?"

"Also history," I said, "and famine and hunger and poverty and the government eighty years or so ago. Plus, families living far away from each other and how they suffered and no one helped them and parents dying and children who didn't have much and how a poem makes you think and feel things with almost no words. That's pretty much all, though."

"You might have led with that," Mr. M said, not pleased. "Good to know you actually read it." He twirled on his heels and moved on.

Actually, the book was great.

But it was somebody else's life, not mine.

At the end of class, while I was barely listening and still riding high on my joke, Mr. M slapped his desk and held up a skinny paperback.

"Our next book: *The House on Mango Street*. Anyone know it?"

A couple of hands went up. "Okay, yeah. It's worth reading again, of course. Certainly, I keep finding new things I missed, subtleties, nuances, hues, *et cetera*. And, bonus, it's only a hundred and ten pages!"

Applause.

He held up his hand. "Thank you, thank you. You do have the best teacher. Now, things being the way they are, we'll need parents to okay this one before I can hand it out. I know, I know, but please, by tomorrow, if you would, and you can pick up your copies then. Take a sheet when you leave. Thank you!"

On the way out I took a permission slip, but since I sign a really convincing *Michelle Hicks*, I really didn't need to bother Mom. Talk about bonus.

But the day was long, and as it dragged on, so did

31

I, forcing myself forward like Billie Jo through one of her dust storms. Somewhere along the way my lungs collapsed. They must have—that's how much my chest hurt by eighth period.

———

Wednesday was a blur. I had a headache all day. Something was creeping around my insides and I couldn't imagine eating any food that I wouldn't instantly spew, which probably made it worse. I handed in my forged permission slip for the book and got a copy from Mr. Maroni. He gave me a squinty look, then said he hoped I would have something real to say about it.

"This is often considered more of a high school book, because of some...racy...stuff in it. I don't agree, but that's why we need a parent's permission."

Cool, I thought. Bonuses everywhere.

———

Thursday, I woke up sick and puked before breakfast. I knew it was stress about seeing my father the next day. Mom called school and let me stay home. She didn't do anything either. After breakfast and the grocery store she came back tired. "I'll be better tomorrow, honey. I feel yucky and you know..."

She was trailing off her sentences more and more.

"Sure," I said. "No problem."

"Give me a hug."

She seemed small in my arms. In a little while, she

went upstairs and fell asleep, so I read comics for a bit before remembering that I needed to start reading the book about mangoes. But it turned out to be another hard story to follow because none of these chapters connected either. It must be nice to write a book and not have to make a story. The chapters here were like old-time snapshots lying out on a table. You look at one, then another one. Maybe after a while you recognize people in different photographs. It made my brain tired and I had to keep going back to start over. So I went to sleep, too.

CHAPTER 6
ON THE PLATFORM

Friday morning, the big day. We ate. Mom drove us to the train station. It was six dollars for the day if you parked after nine. They'd leave an envelope under your windshield wiper, she said, and you paid later by check. We crossed the lot and climbed a short set of steps to the platform. It was windy and just the two of us there. She used her credit card at a machine to buy two one-way tickets to New York.

"Off-peak," she said.

"Kind of like us, since last week," I said with a chuckle.

"Not funny, Jeff. No. It depends on what time you go if it's full price or off-peak price. We'll get return tickets at Grand Central"—she meant the station in New York—"when we're ready to leave. No sense buying one or the other until we know which train we'll be on."

"I know," I said. "I've been down to visit Dad. But good idea."

"Every once in a while I have one. I'll keep the tickets with me."

"I'll get a schedule."

"Another good idea."

"We're on a roll."

"I could eat a buttered hard roll right now!"

I laughed. Yeah, we were on a roll, all right. I'd spent so much time with my mom over the last week, we were becoming best buds. If I was a victim because of Mom, I got my quick humor from her, too.

The inside of the old Fairfield station was empty except for a guy running a vacuum over and over the same patch of floor. Was there no suction left or did he just not care? Sliding a schedule from the holder on the counter, I looked at the clock. Train stations and clocks. Like the olden days. Twelve minutes yet.

There was a bathroom. I went in. Closing my eyes, I imagined my father's face as Mom talked to him. He wasn't funny like me. He nodded, frowned, shook his head, stood up, stepped away.

I was washing my hands when the vacuum-cleaner guy pushed in with a sudsy bucket. He had purple rubber gloves on.

"Hey," he said.

"Hey."

Leaving him in there, I snitched a pair of gloves from a box on his cart. I could have asked for them and he probably would have said okay. I didn't, though. I trotted back up to the platform. It was windy there. My mother was perched on the edge of a bench. I walked back and forth, trying to clear my mind of my father's dumb face, which was all I seemed able to think about.

"I'll probably go on Halloween as somebody with rubber gloves. Look—" I flapped them out of my pocket. "A killer surgeon or something."

"Go? Go where? You're too old to go...Look, Jeffie, I don't think I can see him. Your father." She hunched over into her own lap and rocked up again. "Let's just get back in the car. I'll use the tickets some other time—"

"Mom, no. We need to talk to him. He can't go around just living like nothing's happening. He's a father. If we need money he's got to help."

"Tell that to a judge."

A gust of wind blew up the tracks across the platform and she closed her eyes.

"My head hurts from all this, honey. I have a stomachache."

Yeah, I knew what from.

The four bottles she brought home on Saturday were gone already. Only half a bottle per night, she said. More than that and you have a problem the next day. Well, she was having a problem now.

A train roared by without slowing, on its way north toward New Haven. I thought of my grandfather, but he'd stopped working for the railroad long before the new cars replaced the old ratty ones.

"Did you know," I said, trying to get her off this kick, "that they take old train cars and dump them in the water to become reefs? Somebody told me that. Can you imagine? Fish swimming around the seats?"

She wasn't buying it. "And if *she's* there, I'll probably attack her." *She* meant Dad's girlfriend, whose name was Deb. She was one of the reasons Dad left us in the first place. The other reasons, I guess, were Mom and me.

"You won't attack her," I said, watching the end of the northbound train disappear up the tracks. "I'll do it first."

That was a joke, but Mom wasn't having that either. She stood up from the bench, brushed down her jacket front. "Let's get in the car; we're going home. I'll find another way to get some help until I start working again. I know other people. This is a bad idea."

"No it's not," I said, standing in her way. "Or I'll go alone. I need to talk to him. About school and stuff."

"I don't want you going there alone and confronting him—"

"I have to!" There were people on the platform now, and they were craning their necks to see what we were arguing about, or looking at their shoes because they were embarrassed for us.

I lowered my voice. "I need to find out about St. Damien's. And other stuff."

"Why do you even *think* about that place?" she said, not sharply, but like she really wanted to know. "Jeff, what for?" Her face was red, tired, I don't know what.

"Mom, why don't you give me the tickets and go home? That way I won't need money to come back. Dad will give me lunch. I know where he lives. I'll walk."

"You will not!"

Our train whistled from down the track toward us, and people started jockeying into position. They seemed to know exactly where the train doors lined up with the platform. I squirmed into the nearest bunch, but Mom grabbed my arm and started back toward the stairs to the parking lot. "Come...on!"

The train rolled slowly along the platform, then stopped. Something bad came over me. I pretended not to struggle and went halfway down the stairs with her and then I swatted the handbag out of her hand. It spilled down the steps. A woman saw this and gasped. It was mean and stupid, but while Mom was clawing her stuff together, I pushed onto the train and hurried back to the next car, then the next, and the train started to move.

CHAPTER 7
MOM

I'd done it.

Except I hadn't.

Two minutes after I'd slid into a seat, there was Mom, storming down the aisle toward me, all a mess and steaming like a lobster. Her face was practically purple; her lips were squashed together. She wanted to smack me—I know she did—but not in the filled car. She nudged me hard into the window seat and plunked down next to me.

"That was mean, Jeff. Very mean." She was teary and wiping her eyes.

"I need to see him." The way we talked, we didn't do a lot of dancing around. What to say, what not. We always saw through it, so why bother. Right now, Mom knew exactly why I'd done what I did.

She was silent as a stone for minutes, then looked to see if there was a bathroom in this car. Maybe her stomach actually was rolling over and she had to throw up.

"But yeah. I'm sorry," I said, just to end it.

"Uh-huh."

"It was mean. I'm a jerk."

She sniffed once, then again. "No. You're just..."

"A jerk, I know."

"You're not. Now shut up."

At Green's Farms station, a pack of high school students got on together, in the middle of a round of laughing. There must have been five or six altogether. They were all scrubbed, with expensive jackets and shoes and backpacks, the girls, too, wearing navy skirts and black tights, all standing in the area near the doors.

"They just use the train like this?" I asked, hoping to break Mom's silent treatment.

"I don't know." She barely glanced at them or me. She was still pouting.

"This is how they get to school?"

"I really don't know, Jeff." She arched up in her seat as soon as the train started rolling from the station, then pushed her way into the restroom at the same time as the conductor drifted down the aisle. I pictured my grandfather in his uniform, with the flat-topped hat cocked to the side. That was before, of course.

"Tickets," he said flatly, over and over. He said it again when he got to me.

"My mom's in the bathroom," I said. "She has our tickets with her."

I saw him glance under his hat rim over my head, then nod. So the guy in the seat behind me verified I was telling the truth. Really? The conductor thought I was lying? Did I look like my mom was unemployed? Did I look different already? Or was "liar" always the way I looked? Before he left, he punched holes in a cardboard strip and stuck it in a slot to show there were two of us.

I guess I wanted to prove something, feeling all "out there," like Tom Bender used to say his parents wanted him to be—jumping onto the train alone, going to see my ex-dad. So before my mother finished in the restroom, I slid out of my seat and went up to the rich students. They'd finished their joking by then and were just checking their phones or listening to them.

"Hey," I said.

"Hey," one of the boys said, pulling out an earbud, not smiling, but not with a mean face either. "What's up?"

"What school are you guys going to?" I asked.

"Baines," one of the girls said. "Upper School."

"And you take the train every day like this?" I said. "That's cool."

"Yeah, you?" said the other girl.

I shrugged. "My mom and I are visiting my dad. He's in a hospital in the city. Cancer."

"Oh, sorry," the first boy said. "My aunt has stomach cancer. She did. She just died."

"I didn't know that," the second girl said, touching

41

his arm. "I'm so sorry." She hugged him close, but she wasn't his girlfriend. I don't know why I knew that.

"She was old and had it for a long time. I practically never saw her."

"What hospital is your dad in?" another kid asked.

My brain stuttered. I thought it was another interrogation, to see if I was telling the truth, until I looked into his eyes and saw he was just interested.

"New York...something," I said.

"Presbyterian?"

"That's it."

The kid with the dead aunt nodded. "That's a good place."

"No kidding," I said. "They gave me these last time." I waved the purple gloves out of my pocket. See how quick I am? Not that they were impressed. Rich kids probably have all the rubber gloves they want. But a couple of them smiled.

"Anyway, good luck," I said.

"You too, man," said the boy with the dead aunt, going back to checking his phone. The girl had long ago detached from him and was looking at hers.

You think I'm going to make a point here: They were rich and I was poor so I felt bad. No. I could totally have fit in with them. They were fine. Not snotty or playing superior. They were just on the top of the curve that I was on the downslope of. Next time it could be the other way around, right?

Sure.

Mom was buried in her seat when I got back. She didn't say anything. I tried to sniff if she smelled pukey, but she didn't. It reminded me that maybe not everything shows. Not that my parents were broken up and my mom had no job, not that maybe she just threw up, not that I was a jerk with only one part-time friend.

You'll say you never judge people for that kind of stuff, but that's not true. You judge everything and so do I.

CHAPTER 8
SWEPT AWAY

An hour-plus later, we poured off the train into a sea of bodies. I got separated from my mom right away by three or four guys in suits who danced their way between us.

"Jeff?" she called, but I had to move with the crowd or be trampled. The platform roared. We finally squeezed like toothpaste through a tight arch, into the biggest room I've ever seen.

Grand Central Terminal. You know what I mean. It has a great barrel ceiling about a mile above you, blue like a sky, with faded constellations of gods and animals. That painted sky was pale and cold, and its gods were so far away and getting farther as they faded into the fading blue. It made me feel tiny to be under it, a speck to be swept away by all the noise. Other people raced across the open floor, knowing exactly what they were doing and where to go.

When I turned, Mom wasn't anywhere behind me.

My chest thudded. Was this what it would have been like if I'd left her on the platform before? At the little station was one thing, but here in New York? Now what? I seriously didn't have a dollar in my pocket.

"Jeff."

She was standing by the ticket counter, waving at me, unconcerned. I tried not to show anything in my face.

"That ceiling," she said. "It's something, isn't it?"

"Yeah," I said. "How do you think they clean it?"

She laughed. "Same as I would. Not at all."

I laughed, too. "You need the bathroom?"

"No, you?"

"Nope. Let's go."

———

We didn't know the subway and didn't want to waste money on a cab or a limo, so we walked. It was twenty-something blocks from the station to my dad's apartment, the sideways ones long but the up-down ones pretty short.

The wind came coldly between the buildings both ways.

The city smelled peculiar. Asphalt and exhaust and burned onions and cigarettes and a little bit of fresh air. I couldn't imagine living here day after day like my father did. New York is a giant ball of noise, and after a few minutes you feel trapped inside it. I imagined my lungs dying with every breath.

We were halfway there when all of a sudden Mom

froze on the sidewalk and let people bump and flow around her.

"I can't do this, Jeffie—"

"Not again, Mom, please."

"I'm afraid of what I'll do if that woman is there."

"She won't be there," I said. "I told you. Dad's jerky, but he knows we're coming. Plus, why would she want to see us? It would be so messy. I'm going to tell him straight out what he has to do. The promises he made to us. To me. I have to tell him. We'll tell him together. Mom, it'll be okay."

She closed her eyes as if she were going to cry but didn't, then nodded slowly, her eyes still shut. "You're a good boy."

"The best of the best," I said. I actually hooked my arm in hers and we tramped along the sidewalk like at the end of a movie. After another few blocks, I saw the sign for his street, and acid rose up my throat.

We turned the corner. The numbers went slowly, and the buildings seemed to get dirtier the farther we walked. There was a dead tree in a little squared-off area cut into the sidewalk and a pyramid of garbage bags. Then I found a mop, just lying in the gutter, tooth-marked and smeared with dog droppings. Tell me what happened there, will you? We finally stood in front of his building.

My dad lived above a shop that sold incense sticks and

brass bells and little Buddhas. I knew that, but my mom had never visited.

"Oh lord, lord," she mumbled, shaking her head in disgust. "Let's ring the bell or whatever they have here. Jeff, you go find it. I need to check my face."

While she was doing that in a compact mirror—"You cracked the glass, you little bum. You cracked it when you knocked my bag at the station, you little bum"—I climbed the stone steps to the main floor.

"I'm sorry, Mom. I was nervous."

"And now?"

"Still nervous."

"I'm happy for you. And you're not a bum. I'm sorry."

I laughed it off, because we have such a fun relationship, Mom and me.

Next to the door was a box with the names of the occupants. Dad's name wasn't there, but his girlfriend's was: *D. Franzic.*

"Should I ring?"

"Give me a minute." She smoothed her eyebrows in the cracked mirror. "All right."

I pressed the button.

CHAPTER 9
ANOTHER MOM

A long minute later, a buzz came from behind the door and the lock clicked. I glanced back at Mom and we moved into the lobby together.

It was narrow and dingy and dark and smelled of incense and fuel oil. It was cold, too, almost colder than outside. The walls were stained. Flaps of paint had chipped off, so you could see the plaster beneath. There was a broom in the corner and a dustpan and wastebasket, which I guessed was for the tenants to sweep up the latest junk that blew in from the street.

My heart was pounding fast. I shifted from one foot to the other from nervousness, as if my veins were filled with coffee. When that happens, and it's happened before, I jerk around and do dumb stuff, all electric and jittery. People probably think I do it on purpose. I tried to breathe slowly.

Behind me, Mom was standing with her back against the door.

"You're not going to bail on me, are you? We're going up, right?"

She nodded her head, then shook it side to side. "This is a bad idea. Let's pick up some food. I need to walk around and catch my breath."

She grabbed the door handle just as a door squeaked open on an upper floor. A face peered down the staircase. It wasn't Dad or his girlfriend but a woman older than my mom. She had gray hair. She leaned over the railing. "Hello. Are you here for Deborah? She's my daughter, but she's not in right now."

"No, my dad," I said.

"James Hicks," my mother yelled up hoarsely.

The woman tilted her head, then looked back at something I couldn't see. She came around the railing and we heard her footsteps on the stairs, stopping on the landing above us.

"I'm sorry," she said quietly. "Jim isn't here. I mean, anymore. He left two or three days ago. I have an address Deb asked me to give anyone who came asking. Do you want that?"

"He's not here?" my mother said. "He told me he was here."

"It's just been a couple of days, really," the woman said. She spoke each word so clearly, I felt I was drowning. "Do you want his new address?" she repeated.

"Did he say we were coming by?" Mom asked.

"Not to me, maybe to Deb."

"She threw him out, didn't she? I knew she would."

"We'll take the address," I said. "Please."

The lady stepped down another few steps and handed me a piece of paper. My mom shriveled with each step the woman took—I felt her doing it, creeping back like a shadow—and by the time I thanked the lady and turned, Mom was deep in the corner by the broom. She wouldn't show her face.

"Don't be creepy, Mom," I whispered.

"Do you want me to tell Deb anything?" the lady asked. "You're his son? Jim's boy? Jeffrey, is it?" She sounded like a teacher.

I looked up at her. "Thanks. No. I mean, yes, I am. It's Jeff. But no. You don't have to tell her anything."

"You know," she said, "after everything, I rather liked your father."

My mother gasped. "After everything? Oh my God."

"We'll just get going," I said.

You'll think I was being pretty cool and mature this whole time, handling things like a grown-up might, but I was barely able to stand and was only saying what I'd heard on TV. When I took the note, I watched my fingers shake as if I'd caught one of Mom's hangovers. The lady was so nice.

We went out the door into the wind and Mom put her face into her hands. "Oh, my lord, I can't do that again.

Your father gets thrown out by his girlfriend, and...let me look at that"—she took the note with the address on it, squinted, and nodded—"I knew it, into a stinking worse hole than here. I can't, Jeffie. I just can't go there." Still shaking her head, she turned. "I'm hungry. I have to eat."

"Well, I don't," I lied. "I'm going there."

"No you are not," she said, clutching her bag. "Jeff, I'm not giving you one red cent—"

"I don't need money. I read the address. I can find it. Streets up and down, avenues right and left." I stepped back from her. "People can help me if I need help—"

"You will not do this!" she shouted.

"Oh yes, I will. Go on and eat. I'll meet you at the station around two or three so we're still off-peak. I'll tell you what he says."

I said all this walking partly backward from her, partly forward to keep myself from bumping into somebody. She called after me, but she was crying and it came out muffled. I saw her take a step toward me, then freeze, then just watch.

I watched her, too, until I got to the end of the block, then I turned the corner and was gone.

CHAPTER 10
THE APPLE

By this time the sun was high up, but hidden on the back sides of buildings and dropping angles of light along the sidewalk. It was cold but not freezing. The windy streets actually calmed me, pushing me forward and back at each crossing. I was glad I had my backpack. It kept the cops off me. I looked like one of those rich students hopping around between classes. I was feeling all right.

I was all right, I mean, until I came within three blocks of his new apartment and realized my brain was twisting in knots.

First of all, my dad's old apartment wasn't where he was living. So, was he dodging us? If he *wasn't* dodging us, he hadn't called Mom to tell her the new address, which meant that he *was* dodging us. Except he gave Deb and her mother his new address, so maybe he wasn't. Unless he just forgot we were coming, which was more likely and worse, because it meant he didn't care. See me or not see me—it didn't matter.

I slowed my steps. "So what's the point?"

A sharp dusty wind gusted down his street, blowing my words away. I ducked into an entryway to get out of the blast and nearly trampled a guy crouched on the doorstep.

"Sorry," I said, and made to move on, but he reached up and held out an apple in his dirty fingers.

It was weird. I wanted to run but he wasn't asking for anything. While I gawked at him, he buffed the apple on his sleeve and held it out again. His eyes were milky when he looked at me. "I got it at the kitchen," he said. "Too much acid."

He didn't seem threatening or "off," so I took the apple.

"Thanks. I'm here to see my dad."

He folded his arm back into his coat and tucked his head into his collar like a bird. His shoes were different. One was brown leather; the other was a sneaker.

I stepped back into the wind and walked the rest of the way, eating the apple before tossing the core into a trash bin and wondering how fast someone becomes a bum. How far do you have to fall to eat in a soup kitchen? Was I already on my way to being a bum? A jerky ex-father, a jobless mom who likes wine, doing lousy in a school I hate?

How many steps do you need?

———

Dad's building was on the north side of the block. Four stories, dirty brick. Sucking in a couple of breaths to try to calm myself, and failing, I climbed the stairs to the front door. My legs felt like lead. There was a list there, too. *Hicks* was scrawled under another last name. A roommate? I pressed the buzzer. Apartment 404. There was a little microphone grill, so I expected him to answer, but he didn't.

"Dad, it's me," I said into it. "Dad?"

Just static, then nothing for seconds while I stood there looking like a junior bum.

I rang again.

I rang a third time.

There was no buzz in response, but the door clicked. I entered the tiny lobby. It was neat, swept, warmer than the first. I took a shoe box of an elevator up to the fourth-floor landing and followed the numbers down the passage.

Before I got up the nerve to knock, his apartment door opened.

CHAPTER 11
ALL ABOUT ERICA

My dad isn't a tall man, but standing there in the door-way he was taller than I remembered. I expected more of a wreck, actually. Pajama pants, barefoot, food stains down a bulging T-shirt. But no. He was clean-shaven, not usual for him, and his button-down shirt was tucked into jeans. Skinny ones. Not wanting to, I smiled. Maybe it takes longer than you think to go from man to bum.

"Hey, Jeff." He gave me an awkward long hug. I remembered that right.

"You look like you're going out?" I said.

"Well, yeah, soon. But Colleen called. Deb's mom." He looked past me into the hall toward the elevator. "Where's your mother?"

"Waiting at the station. She was...wasn't feeling well. But I wanted to come." I stepped inside and saw a pink sweater draped over the back of a chair. I thought of tight sweaters and Courtney Zisky. "Is someone here?"

"Well, yeah."

I felt my shoulders go heavy as lead. "You have a new girlfriend already?"

He closed the door behind me and shrugged a bit. Then he did a little showman wave at himself. "Hey, when you look like this..."

Jerk, I thought. "Uh-huh."

He dropped his hands. "Anyway, she's sleeping. Erica. She's been sick a few mornings, actually." He nodded nervously to the left. "I'd be working otherwise. I guess we're both playing hooky. Erica's one of the reasons Deb and I...Well, you get it."

My stomach did a weird tumble. Yeah, I got it. He'd left Deb for this other woman. I was mad and it came out that way. "Seriously, Dad, what are you, fifteen? You're a grown-up father. What are you doing getting girlfriends like you're young? You're not."

"That's enough—"

"No. First you cheated on Mom. Then you cheated on Deb? You can't even keep the family you left your family for." It came out quick like that, like from a movie.

His eyes iced over, another thing I remembered. "Don't get smart with me."

"Too late."

"Well, just..." He shook his head, glanced around, moved the sweater. "Look, sit down. I have to tell you about Erica. There's something you need to know—"

"I *hate* when people tell me that!" I turned my face away. "If I need to know it, I'll know it. I came to talk to you about important stuff. *Family* stuff. Me."

I sat while he went through a bunch of faces and shifted around on the couch until he sat forward, to be honest and close with me. I felt like spitting on the floor.

"Look, Jeff, I know you're not happy, but you know all this. I stayed at home as long as I could. It didn't work out." He said this with a slice of anger in his voice, but softly, so he wouldn't wake her up. His hands stiffened in his lap. His eyes looked suddenly tired, not bloodshot like Mom's, just tired, as if he wasn't sleeping. "Your mother's not even the point now. You heard what I said about Erica. Lately, she's been pukey in the mornings."

"So what? Mom's pukey, too. *I'm* pukey in the mornings. You get that way when you don't know what's going on."

"You're not that simple, are you? You get it, right?" He nodded to her room.

"I'm supposed to 'get' way too much of what you're saying, Dad." I was suffocating in that room and wanted to be pissy. "So maybe just use your words and tell me."

"Okay, smarty, I'll spell it out. Erica's pregnant. She's not feeling well and is sleeping it off. It started a couple of weeks ago, then she called to tell me the other day and Deb answered and well—"

The inside of my chest went cold. "She's going to have a baby?"

"You *are* a genius. Yes. So that's why I'm here. I'm not a bum, you know."

"No, but we are, Mom and me. She lost her job, and we need help. Money help."

"Right, I know, I talked to her. Check that: I listened to her scream for twenty minutes. But here's the thing—"

"No, no, *here's* the thing. We need money. Mom is late on the rent, and you know she's not going to get another job. Not right away. You know her. She'll try, but she's already started...she's drinking more. Or maybe I just see it more. Anyway, you have to contribute."

That was a legal word, a court word. *Contribute.*

"I do," he said. "I have been, child support. I had a problem over the summer, which your mother is being okay about right now. But I'm trying to send every cent the court told me to. Even if I wanted to do more, I can't. Not with this going on. It's all I can manage. You're not a bad kid"—whatever *that* had to do with anything—"but I can't increase it now. Not more than the court says. It's, hey, it's your mother's duty to have a job. They don't call it wife support." Twinge of a smile. He was proud of that. "Look, maybe in a year or two when things get stable. But not now."

"A year or two? I'll be dead."

"Calm down, Jeff." He stood. "I'm making a pot of soup. You hungry?"

"I hate soup."

"Hold on." He trotted into another room. I heard stirring. He came back, sat down. "So..."

"So...why did you leave us, really? I mean why did you leave us in the first place? It wasn't all Grandpa, and it wasn't all...*Deb*..." I whispered her name.

Deb Franzic suddenly seemed like one of the good people in all of this. And she *was* good. She knew enough to kick him out.

"Was it me?"

He shook his head, then spent time moving his lips, then sighed. "Seriously, Jeff, I don't know how to say this again. It wasn't you—it was never you. But you saw what it was like. Your mom, she likes wine. When she got sad, I got sad, I drank, too, maybe more than she did. When her father died, she really went off the edge. It had started before, but it was all downhill from there. And so quick. Maybe you don't know that—"

"I know she's falling off the edge again, and I don't want to be the only one trying to hold her up. I'm in eighth grade—"

"Exactly!" he said. "It's not your job. There wasn't any future there. In that house. You saw it. You were young, but you saw it. It was toxic, you know? I was drinking too much and suffocating. *You're* suffocating—"

"I'm not—"

"I would take you with me if I could."

59

"I wouldn't go."

"I...I guess I know that. Your mother and me, we fought so much."

I stood up from the sofa. "All parents fight. Houses are too small *not* to fight whoever you're living with. I fight with Mom. But not everybody takes off."

"Right. Look, that's done. I'm sober now. Almost two months. Since I met Erica."

Sober. That explained why he looked as good as he did.

"I'm not going to argue it all over again. I just want to tell you that I'm making a change. We're moving out of the city, Erica and me. Fresh start."

I didn't see that coming. "Moving? You can't. Where?"

"Florida. In a couple or three days. Erica's parents live down there."

You don't want to hear the rest. Stupid forty-five-year-old father with skinny jeans and a baby. His head was a stupid solid rock. He didn't hear a word I was telling him. He just said what he wanted to say and it was meaningless, so I won't bother repeating it. Except this bit, when I moved to the door to leave.

"Jeff, wait," he said, reaching out but not touching me. "When you go off someplace, sometimes you see where you are better, you get what I mean?"

"Uh...no, Dad, I don't *get* what you mean. I know you're not coming in with money for us, that's obvious. You'll need it for diapers."

When he drew in a sudden breath of air, I couldn't tell if he was getting ready to smack me or cry. Neither. He smiled. It was a dumb smile, like he knew the moment I got up that he was getting himself off the hook.

"It's like you're in a different place," he said. "And you see yourself better when you're in that different place. Without all the noise around you, everybody talking, drinking, getting mad...without all that, you see it better. You see *yourself* better. The way you're living. The way your life is going. And you can change it. Rearrange things. Leave. Clear all the noise out. Clutter, that's what it is. Clutter. You understand?"

Sure, I understand. You're illiterate. And I'm clutter. I said, "Uh-huh."

"I guess I didn't really know when I was with you and your mother what I was doing being a father." He said this as if it was some big piece of knowledge and I should be happy he'd discovered it.

"Then it's too bad you're back in the business," I said.

He punched the couch instead of me. This was always the first reaction of anyone in my family, lash out first. Me, him, my mother. We all do it.

A pot lid clanked, and there was splattering and hissing from the kitchen.

"Hold on, stay here. I'll be right back."

He trotted his skinny legs across the floor and disappeared into a hallway. People are always doing that.

Going into another room. But you know what? After all this time I've figured out a good thing. When people leave, I get to fill up the space myself.

While he was back there, I peeked into the bedroom. I didn't see anything but a slim brown arm sticking out from the sheets.

Before he returned, I was on my way downstairs to the street.

CHAPTER 12
UNDER A FAKE SKY

After stumbling three and a half laps around the main room of Grand Central with Dad's voice sputtering in my head, I finally spied Mom pacing near the escalators. She saw me and shot across the floor and kissed my cheek. She smelled of mustard.

"Well, what did the bum say? I'm sorry. *Your father.* What did *your father* have to say? I should have gone with you. I feel better now." She stood with her feet spread apart, as if waiting for a punch.

"He's moving to Florida."

"What?" she said. "No, don't say that. Jeff? Really?"

"Florida," I repeated. "Palm trees. Alligators. Beaches. He's going. In fact, he's practically gone. But he stayed long enough to say goodbye, because he's such a great guy. Plus, he's sober, has been for two months."

I guess I wanted that to mean something.

She snorted. "So he says."

"But guess what? He doesn't have any extra money to give us. He told me child support shouldn't change because you lost your job."

"The pig! I've already let him get away with too much. And how in the world is he going to move halfway across the country with no money? Tell me that."

"Maybe the baby will fly them down there."

"Baby?" Her face went pale as ice. "Jeff? What baby?"

"His new girlfriend is all *pregnant*." I made the word sound as dirty as I could.

She slunk back against the wall and moaned behind her hands for what seemed like minutes in the huge room. People on the escalator were staring, so I wrapped my arm around her shoulder and scanned for someplace to sit. There weren't any seats that didn't have restaurants attached to them, so we sat on the marble steps leading down to the bathrooms and let people rush around us.

"I don't understand him," she whispered into my shoulder, still sobbing. "Jeff, I just don't understand him. And I'm the idiot who married him!"

"Mom. You're not the idiot. Believe me. He was wearing skinny jeans."

I sometimes get calmer when people around me blow up, and that's the way it was now. As we huddled together, I kept my arm on her shoulder. I smelled mustard again.

"You had lunch?" I said lamely.

"Didn't you? He didn't give you anything? Bum!"
She opened her wallet. "Get yourself something. Here."

Five dollars.

"I had lunch. Plus an apple for dessert. I'm fine. Put it away."

Swallowing my spit and going hungry turned out to be a good thing, because when it came time to buy tickets home, Mom was so afraid to use her bank cards she decided to use cash and really had to scrape the insides of her bag to pull together enough.

When we ran to get the last off-peak train, she said, "This is just for a little while, Jeff. I promise."

As the train rumbled out of the tunnel into the gray light, Mom blinked her eyes dry into her window reflection, and I realized two truly hilarious things about today.

The first was I didn't even mention St. Damien's. Funny, huh, after all that?

The second? I still wanted to love my dad. Inside me, I wanted to.

When I'd seen his face today, the same face I'd been looking up to all my life, it tingled something in my chest. I was drawn to him. Like his girlfriends are, I guess. I hated him, but that came second. Hating him came when he opened his mouth and when he turned and left you. I wanted to love this worthless guy who couldn't wait to be out of the room. How dumb is that?

———

I was just nine when my parents broke up.

There were no quiet discussions behind closed doors or whispers the afternoon my father decided to leave our house. It was the day Tom Bender and I watched *Duck Soup*. There'd been shouting, but not very much. I had stopped laughing long enough to hear one quick, lame firework—"That's it. I'm outta here!"—and he was gone.

The rest has just been the ashes settling down.

CHAPTER 13
HELP ME

This is just for a little while, Jeff. I promise.

Except they don't tell you that once you start sliding, that slide becomes a free fall. You never catch up to how fast your luck runs away. By the time you realize you have to do things differently, those things don't work anymore either.

One of the first to go was comics. Not a big thing, but still. Mom didn't notice that I stopped buying them or asking for them, or if she did she didn't make a deal of it. I've loved comics forever, following the arcs of the stories. Gone. Then every other day I skipped buying lunch. You can't stop altogether or not pretend to eat, because cafeteria monitors might notice and pull you aside. The days I skipped I still brought a paper bag to put on the table in front of me. When I got home, I put my lunch money back in Mom's change purse. She never noticed.

That was actually easy, the food part. School lunches are only so-so to begin with.

Mom had canceled trash pickup and cable and Internet a few days after she was fired. She canceled the house phone, too, but kept her cell phone.

"For job offers. I need to give them a number."

Our car stunk because Mom would throw our garbage bags in the trunk until she found a trash bin to lob them into, but each day she'd come out of the bathroom saying, "How do I look?"

"Great," I'd say. "They'd be idiots not to hire you."

I never knew who "they" were. Clinics? Visiting nurse services? Temp agencies? Maybe there wasn't anyone, not really. She never volunteered facts when I asked. Most of the time, she was cranky or sleeping when I got home from school.

She started shopping for groceries at the cheap-food warehouse instead of the superstore, and she did it on off-hours, when no one she possibly knew would see her going there. I went a couple of times. The people wandered, leaning on their carts and shifting slowly from aisle to aisle like zombies, touching things, considering, putting them back.

I saw people and places I never had before. My shoulders ached so much when I flopped on my bed after school, I realized I'd been hunching all day, like a boxer guarding against a hit he knows is coming.

Mom began selling things she said we didn't need. We would load the car after dark so no one would see and she'd sell the stuff the next day. I didn't want Rich to see us losing our things, so I stopped inviting him over. We hung out at his house or not at all.

I was planning to ask her "Do we have any savings?"— but I snooped out from some bank statements in her room that we didn't. Dad had been paying eight hundred and fifty-five dollars every month for a while, but it dipped in half at the beginning of the summer, which I guessed was why we couldn't afford St. Catherine's anymore. But it was also pretty clear that Mom hadn't expected the hospital to fire her in January. She hadn't saved much: a little over five thousand dollars, which sounds like a lot but went fast. I figured out that monthly checks to a guy named Mr. Andrade must have been rent. They went up two hundred dollars a month in March, when she was job hunting, so the five thousand was nearly gone before she even got the job at Fairchild Manor.

Every few days a letter appeared in the mailbox from a Bridgeport address. They were addressed to her in jagged handwriting but without stamps. Who was putting stuff in our mailbox? One of her old boyfriends? Skip? Ron? I sure didn't open them.

End tables, the coffee table in the living room. Two old wall mirrors. Plant stands. Table lamps, floor lamps.

Air conditioners. Everything became what we could get for it. She had a deal with a couple of pawnshops in Golden Hill. What she couldn't pawn at one, she could at the other.

"The love seat, how much do you think it's worth? And the chairs. As a set they're worth more, right?" she was asking me. "Help me decide."

Help me. Can you imagine your mother saying this to you? I wanted to scream, but I coughed up an answer for her. "Let's sell them together. I think we should."

"Me too," she said, with a nod and a smile. "I love you."

Do you? I wondered. Maybe she loves me because I help her. Or maybe like me she doesn't really know how to love someone. Wasn't it her duty to have a job to support her child?

Sometimes movers came to the house if the furniture she was selling was big. She said she hoped it looked like old things going out and new things coming in. For the world, it was about the way it looked. For us, it was about the dollars. Soon the living room was clear, then Grandpa's old room, which Mom started filling with boxes and trash bags like a dump.

"You don't use your desk anymore, do you? I always see you on the bed."

"Yeah. No, let's do it."

"Great. There's a demand for kids' furniture downtown. They'll take it at both places, so I can drive up the price!"

"Good, Mom. Good."

Our stuff leaving the house was like selling body parts.

CHAPTER 14
THE GIRL IN MY CLASS

Wednesday. Third period.

Keeping my eyes down, I waded through the halls to Mr. Maroni's room. Most desks were filled and the kids had their new books. I searched my pack, but I must have left my copy at home. I hadn't read more than a few pages anyway. Nothing new.

I found a desk in the back, sat, and realized I couldn't breathe.

Mom once told me how she'd been breathless for weeks after Grandpa died. Always trying to get the air inside, always finding it squeezed out of her. My chest was being crushed, too. I felt like crying it all out right there, but instead rubbed my face hard with both hands, then looked up. Mr. Maroni was perched on the corner of his desk.

"All right," he said. "It's been a few days. You've all got your forms signed by a parent, or, as they say, a guardian, so we're good. And you've all finished *The House on Mango Street*, yeah?"

Murmurs across the room. He looked around. Not at me, good thing.

"I'll take that as a yes. A hundred and ten pages, people! So, you have probably figured out that Sandra Cisneros has written a different kind of novel here. Short but deep and resonant. One in which there is tremendous beauty, sharp, even jagged writing, as well as beautiful turns of phrase and meaning, if we're smart, which we are, and take the time to read closely."

"We smart!" a kid called out, and his friends chuckled.

"Indeed," the teacher said offhandedly. "But you don't have to be a great reader. I'm actually not. There's the choppiness, of course, and a few sentences I have to read a couple of times to get the flow of, but it's really... you just have to pay attention. And if you pay attention over the very few pages of this book, you'll read something that will live inside you the rest of your lives."

"Did you give us a tapeworm, Mr. M?"

A few more chuckles and someone gagged.

"No, Sam. Teachers are prohibited from giving out tapeworms until second semester."

He got the bigger laugh.

"So. What I'm saying is that this story might make you feel something that lasts." He cleared his throat, started walking around. "Thoughts to start us off? Tell

73

us something brilliant. Or not. Let's begin a discussion. What did you like about it?"

I was watching him as if from the back row of a theater. Far away and a bit fuzzy. Josh was at the next desk flipping the pages slowly. Short chapters. Titles in big letters.

He raised his hand.

"Yes, Joshua."

"Well, it's a small thing, but I liked when she— Esperanza—was talking about legs and shoes—"

"Ooh! Josh likes girls' shoes!" someone said.

"Zip it," Mr. Maroni snapped. "Josh, go on."

"What I mean is, it's like what girls think. Or these girls, anyway. The stuff they say when guys don't hear them. The lemon shoes and red shoes and pale blue ones. The long legs. It's like listening in. Like overhearing."

"Yes. Good. You *are* listening in, yeah? Her voice is so close, the narrator's, so close to your ear. She allows you to hear and see what she hears and sees. Good call, Joshua."

He crossed the front of the room, then returned. "Are there parts that made you feel, mmm, emotions? Or that serious things are being touched on in the middle of all the colorful life that's going on, shading it in different ways?"

No one. He ran his eyes over us, one by one. Still no one. I felt nervous for him.

"Well, how about this? The title, right? *The House on Mango Street*. Setting aside for the moment whether there actually *is* a street with that name, what is a mango?"

"A fruit!" someone said. "I think." Some laughs.

Mr. Maroni started roaming again. "Yes! A fruit. And what does a fruit do? What does every fruit do?"

Colin Anderson looked around to make sure I was listening, then said, "Sit in a bowl?"

It was the kind of thing I would have blurted out last year in Mrs. Tracy's class. Now I listened to someone else say it. Poor Colin. It died in silence.

The teacher grinned sadly. "No one? Anyone?"

You're thinking the poor kid would suddenly throw his hand up and prove his brilliance and everybody would love him by his totally appropriate and sensitive answer and give him all kinds of love and money, right? Nope. I just sat there.

Someone shifted in the front row.

"Well..."

It was the girl who had frowned when I read the back cover of that book. Anna. She was tall and quiet. This was the first time I remembered her saying anything at all.

"Yes?"

"Well, fruit ripens and is good for a while, then it starts to rot and you can't eat it. I think that's why she calls it that. Mango Street. Because by the end, she wants to leave it behind. The house, the street, the neighborhood. It's not good anymore. She needs to go. I mean, that's not the only reason to go, but I think she also means 'mango' to be seen like that, as a metaphor. Maybe."

There was a long moment of nothing, no fidgeting, no talking, nothing.

"Exactly right," Mr. M said. "At least that's what I believe, too. Along with everything else, the word *mango* does act as a metaphor, doesn't it? Hannah, go on."

So. Hannah. Not Anna. Hann...*ah*...

"Okay, so..." She cleared her throat. "Esperanza spends the whole book telling you about where she lives, about the people, the color, the clothes, the danger, the humor, everything. It's like the ripe part of her life. Full of so many things. But it can't be forever, right? And then you realize that she's also saying goodbye to it. She's been saying it since the beginning, but we only see it at the end. She wants us to know everything she knows before she leaves it...."

She stopped, shifted her shoulders, and turned ever so slightly to the class, and her braids moved across them. Goddess braids they call them. She was four seats in front of me and two seats over.

"It's her life," she said. "Esperanza tells you so much of it. Dark parts. And funny parts. I laughed out loud, my dad thought I was on my phone—"

Giggles here and there. Josh laughed to himself. "Yeah."

"And it made me so happy when she rides the bicycle. I've done that, three of us on one bike? That made me cry, actually. And when she says about her 'sad red house, the house I belong but do not belong to.' Doesn't that kill you? And when she and her friends drive into..." She searched the pages for a few seconds. "Into 'a neighborhood of another color,' and they roll up the windows. They roll up the dang windows! Not me, but my dad has told me that's happened to him. It makes you mad and scared. And then, the circle...the circle!" She paused. "Well, I'm talking too much."

"No," Mr. Maroni said. "You aren't."

Hannah flipped the book to the end pages and read to herself while we watched her. "This part...'When you leave you must remember to come back for the others. A circle, understand? You will always be Esperanza. You will always be Mango Street. You can't erase what you know. You can't forget who you are.' My gosh, how beautiful is that? And true. We *can't* forget. But then, listen...the last page."

Everyone turned to the end of the book. Josh held his between us.

" 'One day I will say goodbye to Mango. I am too strong for her to keep me here forever. One day I will go away.' So it's like, yeah, we can't forget, but we can go away. It made me cry, but mostly it made me happy. It *makes* me happy."

She paused to swallow and push her braids back. My stomach growled, and Josh whispered, "Whoa!" but my eyes were on her.

"It means I'm not stuck here. I'm here right now. I might even love this place now. But someday, when it's not right, I can leave. I won't stay forever. This isn't everything. I'm not stuck here."

She moved her hands over her cheeks, then set them down on her closed book.

The class was stone silent. You could hear the air. The light from the window.

The kids looked up from their books to see Mr. M's reaction to this speech that most of them probably hadn't even understood. I didn't, not all of it. I just watched Hannah twist in her seat, embarrassed at how the quiet seemed to go on.

And Mr. Maroni?

His face told you. He wanted to shut it down right there. Drop the microphone, turn off the lights, leave the room, his job was done.

"Yes," he said softly. "Hannah, yes."

His eyes were glistening under the lights. What more could anyone say after that?

The old Jeff might have said, *Great. Done. What's our next book?* for a laugh. But I was as quiet as everyone else, watching Hannah settle and resettle in her seat.

Going over what she'd said, this double sense of hope

and hopelessness went through me, laughing and crying at the same time. My ears buzzed with the words.

I won't stay forever. This isn't everything. I'm not stuck here.

Her voice was like a current of water pulling me.

Where, I didn't know, but somewhere else.

I was sweating bullets.

CHAPTER 15
WE WON'T BE THE POOR PEOPLE

I'm not stuck here.

The very next morning I thought this might actually be true, because when I sat down for breakfast Mom smiled big and told me we were taking a vacation.

"Not like I said when I lost my job. A real vacation!"

This was hands-down crazy to say when you're running toward a cliff. My cereal spoon froze in front of my face. "Wait, what?"

"It'll be a little break," she said. "We really need one! A short trip to get us out of ourselves. And it will barely cost us anything!"

At first, I didn't buy it. She must have schemed out something, a plan she wouldn't tell me, but I couldn't tell right away what it was, so I shoved the spoon in my mouth and played along.

"Cool. Where?"

New Hampshire, she told me. A place we'd been to a

couple of times when I was young. It was off-season, she said, so she was able to book a great deal for the weekend. Off-season. Off-peak. Off-hours. That was our new style.

"Are you saying *this* weekend?"

"Yep! It'll be so far from our life and troubles, Jeffie," she said, "it'll be like starting new, never mind that after two days we'll be back. We need the change. I've been making all kinds of calls. After school tomorrow. It's all set, honey."

"A vacation like the old days? Really?" I said. "We like this!"

Then she blew me away again.

"Let's bring your friend Rich, too," she said, getting his name right. "Why not? It'll be fun. The big lake there. Maybe we can even spend time on the beach—in October! We can pay for him, too. We need to lose some stress. And eat big. Mmm, lobster rolls! They're always in season."

"Seriously?" I said, still not believing it. "We won't be the poor people?"

Her eyes flashed like lightning. "Don't you *dare* say that!" A second later, she walked it back. "Anyway, we won't be this weekend. Call your friend. Here."

So I called Rich on her phone, and he flipped out. "Yes, yes! Mom, hey, Mom!" You could hear him screaming four blocks away.

The sun was bright and big and the sky deep blue Friday morning when I looked out. It would be a good driving day, Mom told me, and not too cold.

School was school. Nothing big happened. Hannah went back to being her quiet self in class. I saw her in the hall once and she looked at me with her brown eyes and nodded, but she didn't say anything, of course, since I was just a face. Still, after she had read that bit in class, the book seemed like *her* book, so I wanted to read it in case.

In case what? Who knows?

After I got home, I packed my stuff and the book, which I found—because there might be a slow hour—then ran around putting lights on timers. I checked the mailbox and found it empty except for two of those strange letters. I brought them in, but Mom marched them right back out again unopened. Rich's sister dropped him off around four, and I had to herd him into the car so he wouldn't see our bare rooms. I tossed our packs in the trunk and bounced in after him while Mom slid behind the wheel and adjusted her mirror.

"All set?" she said, smiling in a way I hadn't seen since she lost her job.

"Set!" Rich announced, like it was a roll call.

"Set!" I said.

"Road trip!" Rich yelled, and I yelled it, too.

———

82

It was just past twilight a little over four hours later when we limped into Silver Beach Resort practically on fumes because Mom didn't want to buy gas until we got into New Hampshire, since it was cheaper there.

Silver Beach. Google it. It's nice. I snitched a postcard at the desk to help me remember. Besides the long, low motel building, a half dozen pink cottages sat side by side on a sandy wedge of beach.

Off-season, it's cheap, Mom had said. *They're happy to have us here.* She'd gotten us one of the two-bedroom cottages facing the lake, a square flat-topped pastel-pink box that looked like a birthday present without the bow and had black windows you couldn't see inside. After all those years it reminded me that my mom and dad and I must have driven past Silver Beach when we'd spent my fifth birthday in this part of the state, then we'd come home to find Grandpa coughing his last few breaths.

Rich loved the cottage right away.

"This is so cool. Not only pink, but on a lake."

"And nowhere near home," I said.

Mom unlocked the door. The cottage was dark inside, but we poured in, dumped our junk, and opened the back door onto the beach and the huge lake.

Rich said, "Oh, yeah! This is what I mean!"

He texted his parents a picture, saying he got here okay.

The lakeshore was empty and cold. There were a

couple of lonely beach umbrellas and the smell coming off the lake was a combination of boat fuel and wood smoke.

While Mom unpacked, Rich and I sat on the sand until the stars were fully out and Mom called us inside to get ready to go out and eat. Lobster rolls were crazy pricey so we ordered burgers. We talked about maybe seeing a movie tomorrow night. Everything was open to us. Everything was doable. Everything was everything.

Tired from driving, Mom sat in one of the outdoor chairs on the little patio and smoked two cigarettes.

I tried not to think about going home, tried in my mind to be there at the lake, with the trees, the water, the little curve of beach. I tried.

The television in the cottage was all right, a half dozen local cable channels, which Rich and I made fun of while my mom stretched out on the saggy couch. She said we'd have a big day of fun tomorrow, and Rich believed her.

In the room we shared, Rich propped himself up in bed, reading some of my old comics, part of them aloud, but without the voices I used when I read them. I tried again to read *Mango* but kept drifting away. Skimming, I found a part where people who get lost in her neighborhood are afraid they'll be attacked by people with knives, and I wondered if that was a metaphor or real. Either way, it was a hot story, a summer story, a city story, and it was cold here, so I didn't get far. Other things weren't right.

The smell of gasoline for one. The dark closing like a lid over you. The big flat black lake that went on forever.

Finally Rich decided to call it quits, pushed the comics to the floor, and turned his face to the wall. I peeked out from our room and saw darkness under Mom's door. Turning off my lamp, I slid under the covers and looked up. There were three slash marks of light across the dark ceiling from a spotlight on the beach. They flickered out at one AM, and I went to sleep, too.

CHAPTER 16
SATURDAY

I woke early on Saturday morning, our first real day there. My back ached from the saggy bed. I listened. Mom snoring, Rich still on his side, breathing slow breaths. I rolled out, slid on my pants and sweatshirt, and washed up quietly. It must have been a little after six. Opening the door let a slice of cold air into the room. I grabbed Rich's jacket off the back of a chair and was out quickly and closed the door. I listened. No sound from inside.

Wrapping his jacket tight around me, I crossed the sand to the water and stood in the wind, staring out at the lake. At that time of day, with the sun just coming up, the wind was clear and sharp and piney. The pink light hadn't cleared the tops of the trees and overhead the sky was still solid blue but with no stars. I walked to the end of a concrete pier and just breathed. I heard Hannah talking like she did in class. Softly, like she was telling a secret. *It makes me happy.* I tried to feel that.

A rowboat drifted past the pier, a rope trailing on the surface behind it. One oar sat inside the boat. I watched it being pushed slowly by the wind for a few minutes, wondering how far it would go before something caught it up. You don't see rowboats around Belmont Street. I was trying so hard not to think of home, but there it was.

Our mess was four hours and two hundred and fifty miles away, and I really wanted to leave it back there and find myself here—*here*—if that's even a thing. But it probably wasn't. She might think so. Hannah. Except I didn't know her at all.

I looked down. The water was oily and black in spots. The rowboat was floating farther out. Rich would be up anytime, then my mother. I fished into my hoodie pocket and found the hotel postcard. I scratched a note on the back and tucked it in the cottage door.

Be back soon.

Then—I can't even say why—I lied and added—*With doughnuts!*

I trekked up the main road and down one of the bumpy roads that led off it. Old pavement pretty soon gave way to packed dirt, then woods and water. Being in among the trees, which were like huge Christmas trees, I smelled not lake water, but the brown needles on the ground under my feet. It was calm there. Cold in the shade, but calm and stone quiet. A few minutes of that deep silence, and I realized I could be happy.

"Hey."

I turned around twice before I saw her. The girl must have been five or less. She stood half on the step of a low cottage, half propped to keep the side door open. The cottage was nearly hidden in the trees. There was one of those new double-size Jeeps, with a bike rack, parked in a dirt space next to it.

"Hey," she said again, opening the door wider. She had pigtails and wore an unbuttoned winter jacket and rubber boots. I could tell from the look in her eyes that I'd surprised her. Grandpa said that when he was little people used to invite strangers into their kitchens for food because they were wandering around hungry. I wished I had a candy bar or something to munch to show I wasn't a bum like that.

I gave her a smile like a friendly person. "Hi," I said.

"Get off our road."

I wasn't sure what I heard. "Sorry?"

"This is a private road. Get off it. Mom!" She disappeared inside the house, the screen door clacking against its frame. I didn't move. Was I waiting for the mother? Maybe I thought she'd apologize for her snot of a daughter.

The mother came out, pushing aside the screen door like she wanted to unhinge it. She was in a bathrobe with bare legs and slippers.

"Are you the one who stole our boat?"

"Boat? What boat—"

"This is a private court. Are you lost?" she said, half breathing in when she said it, as if she were nervous or afraid. "You need to turn around and go back up the road."

"I wanted to see the water," I said. "We're up at Silver Beach—"

"Then if you stole our boat, we'll know where to find you. Right now, there's a sign. This is private. My kids are out here and other kids...so would you please..."

She swirled her finger in a sharp circle. I got it. It meant: *Rotate. Get yourself out of here fast.* It was like a slap across my face.

She didn't raise her voice. It wasn't that. It just shocked me how quickly she would go there. *I don't like you, Rich's friend.* The old life I thought I could leave for the weekend was right here with me. I was a bum, after all, and she could smell it. Her brat could smell it. I was stuck here. I bring *here* wherever I go.

So I turned around. I walked up toward the road, but after a couple of steps, I turned back. Her eyes were still fixed on me, narrowed like gun barrels, and she was holding her daughter's shoulders tight. I knew I shouldn't have, but my hand moved up in front of me and I gave her the finger.

She made a noise in her mouth and called a name—Donny or Johnny or Honey—so I ran the heck out of there and across the main road. When my pants started slipping, I stopped to cinch my belt, and a passing truck that wasn't anywhere near me honked and swerved and kept on going.

Donny or whoever came a few seconds later. I heard him running. I imagined a beard and a flannel hunter cap and a shotgun, but I didn't look, didn't show my face. He hurried up the dirt road after me, but I was already weaving my way across a sales lot of canoes and kayaks and ducked into a bait and coffee shop, slowing my steps as soon as I entered. I watched from the window.

The guy wasn't a hunter, but a hipster, clean-shaven, in sneakers, glasses, and chinos and a green polo shirt. He walked purposefully across the sales lot of the boat rental place, then straight over to Silver Beach because I'd told his stupid wife that that's where I was staying. He would trace me to the cottage and make a mess for me.

All because I gave his wife the finger.

Why come bouncing out of your cottage in your bathrobe like that? Why be so rude? Did I really look dangerous? I kept an eye on him through the window, but the guy wasn't at Silver Beach long enough to talk to anyone before I saw him cross the lot again, swiveling his head every which way. He trotted back down his private road to his private court, the jerk. I waited a few minutes, trying to calm down before I went back.

Rich was waiting in the cottage door when I got there. "There's my jacket." He looked me up and down. "Where are the doughnuts?"

"They were out." I ripped the note from the door.

"Aww," he said. "I could use some. Or a dozen."

"We'll go"—my mother said from inside the bathroom—"we'll go to Harvey's. It's a diner in Linton. Jeff, tell him."

Rich grinned. "Tell me."

"We'll go to Harvey's," I said. "It's a diner. In Linton."

"I hope they have doughnuts," he said. "You got me all pumped for doughnuts."

In my memory, Harvey's was one of those sleek aluminum diners that look like an alien ship dropped from the sky. But when we drove up a half hour later, it wasn't like that at all. It was a wooden box with a peaked roof that I must have gotten mixed up with another diner somewhere else. There were only three cars in the lot.

"Is it open?" Rich asked.

"I see lights," I said.

"You do?" he said with a laugh. "Then you must have hit your head!"

"That's stars," I said. "You see stars when you hit your head. And besides, I don't think this restaurant has any stars."

Rich guffawed.

"No, sir. It's good," Mom said. "You remember, Jeffie. Harvey's pancakes?"

Obviously I didn't, and I was pretty sure she knew I didn't, but maybe this was part of her plan, so whatever.

After we were seated by a hostess who set three menus down in the center of the table, a grouchy high school girl came over with an order pad.

"Mmm?" she said, working her eyebrows instead of speaking. She reminded me of Rich's sister. Either that, or she was related to the creeps at the lake.

"You'll love the pancakes," Mom told Rich.

"Sold," he said. "Double stack!"

I went for a blueberry waffle and bacon.

"Coffee for me, just now," Mom said. Then, after the waitress had taken the menus away, Mom told us she needed to make a little side trip. "You eat. Then in, like, fifteen minutes, order me a couple of eggs—Jeff, you know how I like them—bacon, rye. I'll be back in fifteen minutes, okay?"

"Mom, where are you going?"

"Just sit tight. Have fun. Boy talk!"

"Mom, eww," I said.

She blew us a kiss and left.

CHAPTER 17
MEN

We watched from our booth. She didn't drive away, which was good, but crossed the parking lot on foot, then went down the main road a bit before she turned up another street.

"Where's she going?" Rich said, when our food arrived.

I forked off a corner of waffle. My dad made waffles. It was one of the few things he made. These were better. No they weren't. His were.

"I have no clue," I said.

"Ha-ha, you're clueless."

Not funny, but he was right. She'd had a look all morning when we were getting ready, a worried but sly expression. It reminded me of her "pulling one over" face, but I'm usually involved in that, and this time I wasn't.

"I'm not sure we've ever been here before either," I said. "I don't remember this diner. She's up to something."

"But whup?" His mouth was full.

"I'll be back," I said, standing up. "Hold down the table."

In my head I heard a voice say *Is it going to fly?* but Rich wasn't quick enough to say it. He just gawked at me, his fork halfway to his mouth. "Don't leabe me here."

"Eat some of my waffle if you want. I'll be right back."

He swallowed. "I can have your waffle? I could, you know. I'm super-hungry."

"I'm not. Leave me two bites."

Skulking along the road she'd disappeared on, I finally spotted her on the front step of a small, shingled house surrounded by hedges. I snuck behind the one nearest the door, heard the bell, and crouched to listen. Even before anyone answered, my brain came up with the name Ronald Innes. It fell on me like a ton of bricks that her former boss-slash-boyfriend must live there.

That was why Harvey's for breakfast. That was why the whole thing.

A man appeared and squeaked open the screen door. He was about her age or a couple of years younger. I guess she expected him to recognize her, because she sort of presented herself on the step, not saying a word. He finally spoke.

"Mickie!"

He hugged her up the final step onto the porch and invited her to sit on the sunny bench. They started talking. I crept closer until I made out some words, then froze.

"Honey, you should meet my husband."

It wasn't my mom who said that.

She laughed. "Yeah, sure, Ron. Listen, I was wondering, I'm in the area until tomorrow, and I thought maybe—"

"Bob," he called over his shoulder. There was no response. "Bobby!" he called louder, then added to my mother, "We've been married, gosh, almost two years."

I did not see that coming. Neither did Mom.

"You're...Ron, what?"

A second man appeared in the doorway, half inside, half out. He had a sleepy smile on his face as if he'd just woken up. He stepped onto the porch and you could see he was wearing some really wild pajama pants and a T-shirt with a potbelly under it.

"Bobby, this is Michelle Hicks. But call her Mickie, right, Mickie?"

Mom said nothing, just sat there as the other guy put his hand out.

"Bob Dunne," he said. "Pleased to meet you, Mickie."

"Come in and have coffee with us," Ron said. "Have you eaten?"

Mom stood up and backed quietly down the steps. She wobbled. I almost burst from the bushes to catch her, but she managed to steady herself.

"No," she said, and I saw her stiff smile in profile now. "No, no. I don't want to impose. I'm happy for you. Really! I didn't know you were married. I was just in the area. My son is waiting for me. His friend. They're waiting...."

"Bring them over," said Ron.

"Absolutely," said Bob, more awake now. "I brew a good cuppa. I sure need some. Come on in." He reached out his hand again, but she was already on the walk, half turned toward my hedge.

"No. Thank you," she said. "No. I'm so happy for you. I'll send a gift."

"Call me!" Ron called out. "If you come up here again. Good to see you!"

Her eyes were wide and dark as if she'd seen a horrible accident and wanted to unsee it. I scooted away through some backyards, then ran to be at the restaurant before her. When I walked in, I found Rich talking to a policeman.

He saw me and pointed. "There he is. My friend."

Sucking up a breath, I trotted over. "Sorry," I said. "I needed to ask my mom something. She's just coming back from the car."

The cop started shaking his head when Mom hurried in, calling, "I'm so sorry, so sorry." She was flushed and looking back and forth from me to Rich to gauge what we'd said to the policeman so she could try to slip into whatever the story was. She did great. "I'm so sorry," she said for the third time, "it was just a few minutes, after all. I needed something from the car—"

"People see things, you know," the cop said. "They report them now."

"I know, Officer," she said in her most regular voice. "They're thirteen, both of them, and they knew I was just going to the car."

The cop nodded a bunch of times, doubtful, but he took a good look at us and finally bought the story. After talking with the grumpy waitress and the hostess, he left with a coffee to go. Mom paid without eating, and we were silently back on the road to the cottage, which, the moment we got inside, seemed so much smaller than before.

Rich said he had to use the bathroom right away, so Mom and I sat outside the cottage. Because the sun was in and out, it was cold, but not bad. The lake was calm and gray and long.

"I was just out taking a walk," she said. "I had gas."

"It's cheaper here," I joked.

"No. I meant—"

"I know, and it's way too much information," I said.

She'd probably hoped something might happen, some miracle during the weekend away from our crummy lives. Probably all the way up to his front door, she hoped it would. She was looking for a bailout, or a handout, or whatever, and thought of this guy, how he was once her boss and how she liked him and she felt a spark, but she found there wasn't any spark, and was totally embarrassed. I would be. In shock, too.

"To tell you the truth, I popped in to see an old friend from work," she said finally. "Five minutes, that's all. Police make such a fuss."

I played along. "Huh. A guy? And he moved up here?"

"I knew he moved up here a couple or three years ago," she said. "It's not like we kept in touch or anything. Not like that."

No kidding you didn't keep in touch.

"So is that why we came up here, Mom?"

"No! No. Not really." Then she sighed and stopped pretending. "I don't know what I was thinking, Jeffie. I *wasn't* thinking, that's all. We were a little close, once, him and me. I thought we were. I was wrong, I just found out." A pause. "The air is beautiful, isn't it?"

"Colder than home."

"The truth is... is..." She snorted, a sound between crying and laughing. "I went to see Ron. My old boss. He lives near there. But he's married now. I had no idea."

I guess I could have been funny, joke about Ron and Bob, but what was funny? They got married. They seemed like okay guys. Cool little house. Besides, what was funny about how disappointed Mom was?

"Sorry," I said.

"Oh, Jeff." She breathed and I think the air filled her lungs so much, it pushed on the inside of her eyes, because when I looked her face was wet.

"Hey, Mom, don't. Rich will see...."

"Your grandfather..." She sniffed up. "Grandpa...he was...everything..."

Why she mentioned him right then, I didn't get at first. Then I remembered *Daddy, oh, Daddy,* and that Grandpa was probably the last decent man she knew. It sure wasn't my dad. Grandpa's face came to me, his old white face sunk into the pillow.

"He was everything," she said.

"I know. You miss him a lot. Me too—"

"I mean," she said, "he was *everything.* So many things in his life. He was a roofer. He paved roads. He could do anything with tools. He put in our kitchen cabinets, did you know that? Your father wouldn't. Couldn't. Your father doesn't know a two-by-four from a Phillips head. Worthless. Your grandfather was in the army in Alaska, did he ever tell you? Oh, you were too young. He was a radio operator, doing spy things."

"Get out. Really?"

"It's near Russia, so he had to. After that he hiked back from the army. It took him three months, living in the wild. He was in California for a year or two, where he dug graves in churchyards, then Texas. He never lived in the same place twice. Always moving. In Chicago he worked on trains, then trains in Baltimore. That's where he met Mommy, where I was born. We moved to New York after that. All for trains. He loved them. Even after the railroad lawyers chiseled him at the end, he loved his trains, loved moving. Until he couldn't move anymore."

"I never knew that. Graves, huh? Maybe I should go as him for Halloween."

She laughed. "You could use the long shovel from the garage. And wear some old clothes. I wonder what he'd think of us, of me, all this—" She stopped short. Her face wrinkled up. "I wish we came to the lake more when we were happy. You know?"

"I know. The last time, remember? We came back and Grandpa was sick...."

She covered her face. "Oh, keep quiet and tell me what we're going to do!"

I could have made a joke of that, too, talking with my mouth closed. Instead I slid my arm over her shoulders like a man would. "Mom. We'll figure it out. We'll deal. We don't need much. Practically nothing. Two rooms. We kind of proved that."

"Nothing but each other," she said. "You're my silver lining, right? A real blessing."

It didn't sound great. In fact, it sounded weird and bad. But I nodded. "A team."

There was the sound of gravel behind us, and Rich

was there. "I just pooped twice. I mean, I thought I was done, then I wasn't."

"What is with the too much information today?" I said.

"Sorry, I think I caught something. Maybe from the pancakes. They were a little runny in the middle."

I laughed. "Now *you* are."

"Mrs. Hicks, do you think we can go home soon? Like now? I think I'm sick."

I surprised myself by still having my arm on Mom's shoulders in front of Rich. I felt her shoulders move when she nodded okay.

"Sure, honey," she said. "We'll pack up. It'll probably rain tonight anyway."

"Okay," he said. "Sorry. I might have to go again before we leave. Oh, man." He pushed back into the cottage, leaving the door open.

I snorted. "Maybe we should have had doughnuts instead."

"Because that would have made all the difference," she said with a sigh.

Then she wiped her eyes, kissed my cheek, and we went into the cottage.

CHAPTER 18
THE KEY TO NOTHING MUCH

The drive back was quiet. Rich tried to keep his insides inside and that took all his concentration. I hated, hated, that we were already on the way home, but a part of me knew this was better. It was a mistake to drive so far and still find *us* there. At least at home we knew who we were. We belonged at home. No surprises. No brats.

When we finally got off the highway, it was afternoon, clouding up and getting dark. It would rain after all. Mom drove through town and happened to pass St. Catherine's. The parking lot was empty. I thought about Mrs. Tracy, and I wondered what she'd said in class when I didn't return. Rich told me she'd moved up to teaching eighth grade, so she had to have most of the same kids from last year. When she told them I wasn't coming back, did she put on that serious face she used to when she made announcements? Or did nobody care I was gone? Why would they?

A few more turns and we were on Rich's street.

"Not the great getaway you expected, huh?" I said when we pulled up in front of his house. "Cops and getting sick and all."

He shrugged. "Nah. The cottage was cool. Mom'll laugh when I tell her I stayed in a pink house. Tom and the other guys, too. Courtney's pretty friendly to me now, too—"

My neck froze. "Don't tell Tom about this. Don't say *anything* to him. You hear me?"

His eyes went wide. "Whoa. Okay, I won't."

The door opened. It was his mother. She said something when I left Rich on his doorstep. By the time I was sorry for screwing up the last few seconds of the stupid weekend, the front door had closed behind me. I slumped back into the car.

"What do you care about your old school people?" Mom whined.

"What do you care if I care? And I *don't* care—"

"You're not going back to those kids, and the quicker you understand that—"

"Well, you're not going back to your job at the hospital either, so why do you still drink with your nurse friends like you're still there? I know that's where you go at night. You taught me what I know. You taught me everything. Just drive. Go! I don't want to talk."

That began a deadly silent slow-motion drive back to our house.

Since the mention of my grandfather that morning, his waxy face kept floating into my mind, how his head weighed into his pillow, the words he'd said that made no sense back then.

"Aww, Jeffie," he told me, a string of saliva dangling from lip to lip. His teeth were brown. "It goes fast."

"What goes fast, Grandpa?"

"And only in one direction," he said.

"What goes fast? A train? Your train?"

It wasn't a train, stupid. It was his life. My life. Our lives.

It was actually the little money that Grandpa had saved before he died that got me into St. Catherine's in the first place. Why I can't stop thinking about that place, I don't know, but it all connects. Grandpa helped me start going there, my father helped me stop going there, I liked a girl there, she hated me, I hated Tom Bender, Rich's mother hated me, I loved my mother, she slapped my five-year-old cheek, it all connected.

Somebody had said, *This isn't everything. I'm not stuck here*, but what the heck did she know?

Mom drove the streets without breathing a word. I think she was finally spent, which isn't a joke or a metaphor. She was worn down. Dry. Empty. The meeting with Ron had sucked everything out of her. It also didn't help that I was a royal jerk. I was empty, too, nothing inside but nothing.

The sky was dark blue by the time we pulled into the driveway. When we hauled our bags up the walk, I noticed the lights I'd left on timers were out.

And the house key didn't work.

CHAPTER 19
MY HOUSE

She jiggled the key in the door, wagged it back and forth. "Oh, lord, no."

"You have it upside down."

"My house! I can't get in my house."

"Turn the key around."

She coughed out the words. "It won't work!"

"Because you didn't do it right!" I tore the key ring from her shaking fingers and tried the lock myself. The key went in but it didn't turn. I jostled it around as dumbly as she had. I slipped it straight out and back in. The lock was dead. It wouldn't give.

"Mom, what the heck? Why won't it work?"

Without waiting for her to blubber up an answer, I took the key to the side door, then to the back. Same thing. By the time I was around front, streetlights were popping on up and down the street.

"How are we supposed to have our stuff?" she said

weirdly. "This is where we live! What's happening to me?" She flung her head around as if someone would jump out of the bushes and yell, *Surprise!*

Then she bent toward the front window to read some clue from inside. I did, too. There wasn't any clue. The living room was empty like we'd left it, only black.

"Let me try again!" She rubbed the key between her fingers, because a piece of lint would obviously prevent a brass key from working a brass lock.

"Try the other doors," she said.

"I just did—"

"Do it again!"

This time I noticed the lock on the back door glinting in the light from another house. It was new. When I ran back to tell her this, she was stuttering into her phone.

"Uh-huh? Yes. Yes!" There was rumbling at the other end. "You b-better be!" Her voice cracked and she hung up.

"Who were you talking to?"

"The landlord," she said. " 'I'll be right there. I'll be right there,' he says. Except he was *surprised* to hear from me. As if he didn't expect me to call. What kind of fool is he? He'd better be here soon. That's all I have to say."

She turned on her heel, then wobbled down the walk to the driveway. It was the second time today I'd seen her shaking when she left a house.

It was cold. I shivered. "Should I bring our stuff back to the car?"

"What? No. Leave it on the step."

She beeped the car open and we sat in the front seat, waiting for Mr. Andrade, the landlord. He didn't come soon and when he finally arrived he wasn't alone. Two cars pulled to the curb and flicked off their lights. A small man got out of his car at the same time as a big-chested man in a suit got out of the other one.

"Oh," she whispered. "Him."

"Who is it?"

We went to the front door to wait for them. The little man was the landlord. He was sour-faced and quiet, while Big Chest said he was a state marshal.

"A marshal?" I snapped. "Where's your badge?"

He smiled, but not at me. "Hello again, Mrs. Hicks. You remember me."

"I . . ." She shook her head.

"Yes, you do remember."

"Mom?" I said.

While the landlord said nothing, the marshal fiddled in his side pockets, murmuring something, then handed her an envelope.

She waved it away and wouldn't take it. "You can't do this," she said.

"I can." It sounded like he snickered, then cut himself short. "I did inform you it might come to this. Please take it."

He pushed the envelope at her, and she took it or it

would have fallen to the ground. His hand was already back in his jacket.

"I'm sorry, we have to," said Mr. Andrade. He was short, nervous, shaky. "I need my house back. I don't own lots of houses. Only three. Mortgages, all three. I'm not a rich man, you know? I need my house."

"Your house!" she said. "How can you say it's *your* house? It's *my* house! I just left it yesterday. And you can't lock me out of it. I know my rights! It's illegal! I'll have my lawyers get right on you for this—"

I didn't know how it got so loud so quickly, but Mom turned her eyes on the marshal and kept going. "You know he can't do this! I have rights. You can't surprise us with this kind of thing. There are laws—"

The marshal raised his hands in the air and lowered them slowly. "It's *not* a surprise exactly, is it, Mrs. Hicks? I talked to you three months ago and told you three months and three months is up now. Do you have back payment? And *do* you have a lawyer?"

She didn't answer.

"All right, then, ma'am," he said. "But you are correct—"

"She moved out!" Mr. Andrade said. "I saw it. I looked in the window. No furniture! You moved out. Days ago. I thought you moved out—"

"What?" I said.

"Your furniture. I looked in last week, furniture gone.

I didn't go in, but I looked in. I looked in today. Furniture still gone!"

"You *looked* in our *house?*" I said.

Mom shook her head like there were bees buzzing around her. "No! No! We're decorating!" At that point a police car drove up and a woman got out. "Oh, lord, what's this now?"

A big mess was growing in front of our house. The policewoman had a pretty face, a heavy belt packed with stuff, including a gun. She seemed young.

"You didn't pay me rent," the landlord was saying, "you didn't pay me for five months, not all of it."

"Five months! That's a lie," I said. "A week. A couple of weeks, right, Mom—"

"Yes, weeks," she repeated me. "Not months—"

"Almost five months. Will be five months next week. I gave you all the chances, many chances. I wrote to you. Mr. Barnes here, Marshal Barnes, has seen you and told you. The court allowed you here since August."

"Mom? When did all this happen?"

"You removed furniture," the landlord went on. "You don't pay me. I thought you went. I gave you time. All I have to do is put a notice in your mailbox, which I did do, several times. You knew I did, because I watched your son take in the mail."

"You *watched* my *son?*" she said. "You pervert!"

"Now, ma'am," said the marshal.

"You spent my money!" the landlord said. "If you don't pay me, I can't pay my bank. They could foreclose on me. Not to pay rent is stealing from me."

"That's just...insane," I said.

"No. Not insane," Mr. Andrade said, turning to me, then back to my mother. "Believe me, I'm in trouble without rent. I have bills. We all have bills, Mrs. Hicks. Many bills—"

"Ms!" she said. "Ms. Lewis. I'm changing my name. And I can get it. Just give me a little more time."

"Well, I'm afraid that's not possible," the marshal said, and he motioned to the envelope in her hands. "You are holding a Notice to Quit. Mr. Andrade is right. But you're also right. We cannot lock you out today—"

"We'll lock her out—"

"We cannot lock her out, not today," the marshal repeated firmly. "It's not legal. You have to let them back in."

"An hour to get the rest of your things. I'm sorry."

I went ballistic. "You can't be serious! You can't throw us out. What are we? Who do you think you are? Some kind of—"

"Please, son," the policewoman said, putting her hand on my arm. "Mrs. Hicks, your son. Mrs. Hicks—"

"Hicks was my stupid husband's name!" Mom screamed at the cop. "And don't touch my son. Jeffie, stop. An hour is...it's nothing. I need a month."

"What? Mom, don't say that!" I shouted. "It's our house. We live here. It's *our house!*"

"A month," my mom repeated, lowering her voice.

"A week," the landlord said. "You put the rest of your things in a storage locker. One week."

"Two weeks," she said, with a pleading look at the marshal.

"Mom, no!"

"Two weeks sounds fair," the marshal said. "They need that much time."

Between them they were slicing bits off my life.

"Does that sound fair to you, Mr. Andrade? It does to me. Two weeks? You're a fair man. They have the Notice to Quit. Ma'am, you have the notice, and I will be back. For a third time. I don't come back more than three times. I've never had to. Mr. Andrade has a right to his money. It's like you went into a store and took something without paying for it. It's the same thing."

"You're..." she started, then just shook her head.

I was shaking. Lights were on in the other houses, lampposts, garage lights, cars slowing as they drove past the police car, faces looking at us from the street.

Mr. Andrade threw up his hands and stomped down the walk and back up again. "I have a sign. For Rent sign. I have a right to put it up. On *my* lawn. I'm showing the house. Two weeks? Okay. Two weeks. I'll show the house then."

"I'd suggest you get a storage locker, like the gentleman says," the marshal said quietly. "You don't want us to have to put your things on the curb, do you? You do not. That's not how we want this to happen. Storage locker. There are plenty around. You've already started to downsize, yes? Well, then..."

Mom just nodded, biting her lip not to cry. We watched Mr. Andrade open the trunk of his car and tug out a sign about two feet square. FOR RENT in big red letters on a white background with a telephone number. He pushed it into the lawn next to the sidewalk so both directions could read it. "The neighbors will know you don't pay. Seven thousand dollars. More maybe, if there is damage. That's how much you owe me since June."

"What? Seven *thousand*? Mom, tell him!"

She closed her eyes. "Just give us the new key," she said. "Two keys."

"One key," the landlord said.

"I need my own key," I said. "Sometimes I'm here by—"

Mom pinched my arm, which meant *shut up*. "One key will be fine," she said.

"Two weeks," Mr. Andrade said. "I'm sorry. End of it. Over."

She pushed away from them, dragging me up the walk to the door. When she inserted the new key and opened the door, it came over me again. My legs jerked me around and I gestured at Mr. Andrade. You know what I mean.

The marshal shook his head. "Now, son..."

The landlord just hung his head. He tugged the marshal with him. "No, it's okay," he said. "I understand. I'm sorry for the boy." He beeped his car open and got in.

It rushed through me. I was a bad person. Mr. Andrade's face sank. I practically felt the blood drain from it. He wasn't any different from everyone else. No better, maybe, but no worse. He was miserable. I felt small and stupid.

"Wait...I...didn't mean..."

But his car was already moving.

CHAPTER 20
DAYS AND NIGHTS

Sunday came and went. We barely said a word and didn't leave the house.

The next two days I was a zombie. School, house, Mom, night, sleep, no dreams, school, house, Mom, night, sleep, no dreams.

Wednesday morning I woke up laughing like an idiot.

I'd dreamed about needing to go to the bathroom. I guess everyone has. Maybe it was Rich's problems in New Hampshire, I don't know. I was running around a strange old building, a kind of weird rambling mall, and people were telling me where a bathroom was, and I had to go really bad, but it was far away, through room after room, along corridors, up and down flights of old stairs, and when I finally got where they'd said to go, the toilet was sitting out in the open in the middle of a room like a throne.

People walking all around it.

I tried sitting because I really needed to, but everyone watched me, so I didn't go and asked where another one was. More alleys and rooms and stairs.

Once I found a toilet sitting in the corner of a ladies' dressing room. Women changing their clothes everywhere.

At last I found a school lavatory, a kind of locker room, and I used the toilet there, but when I looked down I had apparently been doing my business on the person who had sat down before me. He hadn't finished yet. I was in a guy's lap and he was mad that I was ruining his pants.

But that wasn't the end of it, because the guy started chasing me from room to room, complaining that I'd messed his pants and he needed clean pants to be where he needed to be, so could I hurry up and clean them? I kept telling him I had no idea how to clean them, but he kept appearing and showing me his pants and saying I had to.

"What the heck?" I said, sitting up in my bed. "What does that mean?"

Dreams are sometimes simply weird and you have to laugh at them because otherwise you'd be scared out of your mind. It was only when the endless stairs and rooms faded from my mind and my bedroom took over that I realized that dreams were one thing, and they could be as strange or funny or dumb as whatever, but I was being kicked out of my house.

Mom yelled, "Bus! Bus! Jeff!"

I didn't know what I was going to do about the bus in two weeks—a week and a half now—when our time ran out, which I still didn't believe was possible, because Mom said she was working on it. But I bolted up, got dressed, and collected my notebooks in, seriously, under a minute. I looked for *Mango Street*, but I couldn't find it. "Mom, where's my book? Why can't I ever find my book? We have a test soon."

"What book?"

"*Mango!*"

"That's a fruit, honey."

"Mom!"

"Maybe you left it in New Hampshire."

"What? Did I? No!"

"By the way, I won't be here when you get home. I'll leave the key under the side doormat. I have a lead, Jeff. On a job. Guess where? At the medical office across from the library. The new building. They need an office manager. Right up my alley."

"Really?"

"This could be it, honey!"

I hoped so, except I didn't really have much hope left. The way things were going I figured our situation was a ball that only rolled downhill.

———

When I got to school, I scanned the classroom library. Not a single *Mango*, which makes it sound like a lousy grocery store. I'd try the main school library later, then the public, if I had to, and maybe catch Mom after her job thing.

Hannah was talking with Mr. Maroni. No, not with him, *to* him. The way he listened to her, frowning and nodding, reminded me of Mrs. Tracy from St. Catherine's, who listened like she was trying to hear whether a person was saying something other than what they thought they were saying. Hannah went back to her seat not looking at anyone.

"So," Mr. Maroni said a couple of times until we paid attention. "Day after tomorrow, our *Mango* test, half the class period, all essay, so that's that. The next book we're all going to read together is *Of Mice and Men*. I'm sure you've heard of it?"

A few hands.

"John Steinbeck, 1937. Gritty, bold, cinematic style, or rather written to be easily adapted to stage or screen, which it was right away. And, continuing our theme of short classics, it's very short. Shorter even than our last one, coming in at a hundred and three pages." He held it up. It was as thin as a cell phone.

Applause from here and there.

"Seriously, I'm not trying to be the best teacher, it just comes naturally. But first, Hannah says that Sandra Cisneros has a great website. Lots of biographical information, letters from her, and you can write to her from it. So, if you want to go further, you have that."

Hannah was sitting in the opposite corner of the room today, near the author posters. She was back to her quiet self after her big speech and looking out the window at some crows.

"You know," he said, "so many things for young people—stories—are supposed to be about hope, right? They feed you this stuff as if you don't know any better. As if you don't look around you. Happy ending, or if not happy, exactly, at least there's got to be a future. Because without hope, kids will break, right? You'll shatter. I don't believe that, and neither do you. I think we might agree that there's a good bit of hope at the end of *Mango*, but maybe not—maybe?—in our next book. No spoilers here, but something to keep in mind—hope or not—as you read this twentieth-century tragedy *Of Many Mice*. Sorry, *Of Mice and Men*. You can finish it by fifth period today, no doubt, but I prefer slow reading, so by Tuesday, if you would...."

Hannah undid her eyes from the crows and turned back to us. While Mr. M went on, I heard her reading in my mind again.

One day I will say goodbye to Mango. I am too strong for her to keep me here forever.

I hoped it was true and not just a metaphor or a

made-up story about made-up things. Either way, I knew I had to read it, the whole book, all hundred and ten pages.

The rest of the school day was a haze of Hannah's face and those words and a pair of arms—not hers, not brown, maybe my mother's—holding me, keeping me there, and the sound of crying as I tried to pull away. I didn't know what that meant, but it made me sad and nervous at the same time.

I took the bus home, flew off down my street, but stopped short when I saw a truck in our driveway. The backup lights flickered on, and it curved onto the street and drove away.

I walked slowly up the sidewalk to my house. I peeked in. No one. The key was on the concrete under the mat by the side door.

Throwing my stuff on the kitchen table, I listened for sounds. Only my breathing. There was a smell of sweat and paint in the air, but too faint to be anything but what a guy might leave behind walking through. I scavenged for food. The refrigerator blew cold air at me while I stared inside at not all that much. Butter. Lettuce. A jar of pickles. A packet of cheese. Rubbery carrots. I ate the cheese and some crackers while I read over the note on the kitchen table, especially the last two words.

Job appointment at 3:30 in town. I'll be home with dinner. Maybe celebrate!

My chest sizzled with something. It was nearly three

thirty now. Could this interview actually be the one? Maybe it would turn us around. We could keep the house after all. Talk about hope. I wanted to be there when Mom handed Mr. Andrade a big check and he backed away, shocked but smiling. Problem solved.

Mom's interview was in the new medical building across from the public library, which had to have *Mango*. It was a classic, right? I went to the bathroom, imagining the interview. When I washed up, the hot water never got hot. The kitchen water either. I wonder how soon Mr. Andrade would fix that. Would he even bother?

Hopping down the front walk, I felt all those other faces go away and there was Hannah in my mind again.

This isn't everything. I'm not stuck here.

CHAPTER 21
THE BLUE HOUSE

The afternoon grew colder as I walked. The sky grayed. There was a straight way to the library from my house, but I didn't take it. Zigzagging on streets I normally don't use kept me off the main roads. I was getting used to the idea of walking distances, but I didn't want to press the idea of a kid alone. Mom's paranoia had rubbed off on me and you never know who's watching.

So I'm pushing ahead on sidewalks and through yards where there are no sidewalks, when suddenly it strikes me that while I wasn't paying much attention to what was around me, my feet were directing me, because my legs suddenly stalled and I froze near the corner of Harrison Street.

Here? Why am I here?

A few more steps to the left and I saw it. Across the quiet short street was a two-story blue house with a charcoal-gray door. A wreath-y sort of thing hung on the door at eye level. I knew the house almost as well as my own. Tom Bender lived there.

How many times had I pulled open that side door with him, set foot into the narrow hall, and stepped into his kitchen, where an island cramped the small floor space. Once when I entered, there was a warm smell of soup and bread baking.

Who bakes bread anymore?

"Let's go up," he'd say. "You have to see the new model."

"Another one?" I'd say, or maybe I just followed him.

Upstairs to the right and left were bedrooms, with a pale green bathroom in between. Maybe it wasn't green anymore. I remembered noticing the peeling ceiling when I looked up once. The room we usually went into had light gray walls, finger-darkened around the light switch. His desk. Packed bookshelves. Rumpled half-made bed. Puny collection of comics. Model cars, all the same car in different sizes: a fat low Cobra, red, white racing stripes, pumped-up tires.

"The most realistic so far." He'd hand one to me, then wait for my reaction.

He must have been in his room that day he called me, crying that my stupid uncle hadn't come roaring into town with his real Cobra, which he insisted I had promised we would ride in. I barely knew what he was talking about because my uncle never follows through on anything and that was also the day Mom dented a parked car because she'd had wine at brunch.

"It wasn't that much," she'd said.

"What, the wine or the dent?"

"Neither!"

Then she freaked out because she was sure somebody would report her. Two seconds later Tom called and screamed at me: "Where's the car? Where's the car?"

That was another great day in my life.

I hadn't thought about the blue house, about coming here, about each street I'd need to take to get here, for months.

So why now?

Maybe that was exactly why I was here. I hadn't thought. The way here was too natural. No matter what I thought of him now, it must have felt right to arrive here. The lefts and rights, the corners, the streets to cross. And it *had* been right for years, coming to his house, being inside it, just being. It was something I did so many times before it all burned to the ground.

A sudden wing of brown leaves flew out of the hedge, blew apart, and sprayed across the lawn. Another. Someone was raking leaves from the side yard into the front. The leaves were mostly down from the trees by now, so it was time. I moved behind a thicker tree to not be seen.

Mr. Bender, hatless in the cold, his jacket unzipped, pawed his rake at the ground, clawing leaves out of the border and across the tops of his shoes. He dug like that for a minute or two, then stopped and looked behind at what he'd collected. His shoulders slumped. There was a ton more to do. He looked the same as last fall, the last time I could remember seeing him.

What I hated was how Tom had turned on me just as things got weird with Mom. She had been slowly losing what I now knew was her *part-time* job at the hospital. She drank a lot of wine, sometimes while Tom was at my house.

And of course there was Jessica Feeney.

Everyone, Tom mostly, wanted me to be all friends with her and thought I was mean for not holding one of her burned hands, not being able to make myself hold it, and for saying what I said. I don't even remember what I said, but whatever it was, it was the end for him. Mom was right. Tom Bender abandoned me. Never mind. Never mind, except that he tossed me away while he was walking somewhere, like I was a weight that tires you to carry.

Mr. Bender was making a real mess, rattling and tearing at those leaves like a mouse in a trap. Cursing at the air, at nature, at himself. I watched him open a tall leaf bag, fold the rim over to keep the sides up, then press his rake into the pile of leaves, squeeze it with his other hand like a set of clamps, and try to empty the whole thing just as the bag folded away from him.

Clumps of leaves fell to the ground. He kicked the bag. He was funny. He'd always been funny. Quiet and funny. I liked him. I wonder if he ever asked Tom why I didn't come over anymore. Maybe he didn't. Should I like him anyway?

My heart flipped when he suddenly glanced over and half raised his hand, but he hadn't seen me, wasn't waving, just sneezing. I was standing so still I was invisible. He propped up the bag again, regathered the leaves, and got it this time.

Score one for Mr. Bender.

He was doing better than me.

In the shadow of the trees, I cut unnoticed to the end of the street and turned toward the library.

CHAPTER 22
OUR SHAME

It was after four by the time I got to the town center. Our car was still in the medical building parking lot, so I peeked in at the office. Mom bounded up from the bench when she saw me. "I'm still waiting," she whispered, then made a face at me. "You look awful. Did you walk from school?"

"From home...the house. I need a book at the library."

She shook her head while tugging out the shoulders of my shirt. "Did you run? You sort of smell, honey. BO."

"Sorreee. The hot water didn't come on, you know."

"I've been keeping the furnace down. I should have told you."

"By the way, there was a truck driving away from the house when I got off the bus."

"No!"

"I didn't go in until it left."

"Stinking rat," she hissed, and pushed my hair

behind my ears. "He said no one would be there after school hours."

"They almost weren't." I pinched a spec of lint off her sleeve. "This top again?"

So many things were going into cartons or in bags that Mom was rotating the same two or three outfits. She knew what she looked like but couldn't do anything about it.

"It's fine," she said. "Look at us. Fixing each other up."

It hit me then how every sentence we said, every word, had our shame behind it. How all the words, by themselves, told the truth of what was going on. Most people weren't listening closely enough, but I knew Mom heard as well as I did. Nothing was regular about this little scene. I had walked too far and sweated through my days-old shirt. Mom's clothes were wrinkled and she was afraid. It was all because we were losing our house. I felt like throwing up.

A door clicked open and a lady waved from inside. My mother nodded to her.

"Go get 'em," I whispered.

She smiled at me and followed the waving lady.

———

I trotted across to the library. There was an empty table in the adult stacks, and I put my pack down. The air was full of those smells you always smell in a public library: the weird sweetness of old paper, brittle cellophane, something like rancid baloney, dust, copy-machine toner, farts—or maybe the baloney smelled like farts—dusty carpets. Every odor was exaggerated and mixed together because libraries never open windows and are always overheated in cold weather.

A single thousand-year-old copy of *Mango* was all that was on the shelf, and it was only there because it was misshelved and you could barely read the worn spine. I flipped through the yellow pages. Nearly every one was underlined and highlighted. Holding it was like wearing someone else's swim trunks.

But I turned the pages anyway, looking for parts to catch my eye. My tongue, like always, formed the words as I read them. I guess that's why I'm a slow reader. It tires you out, your mouth moving while you read, and it looks stupid, so I turned my chair away from the other tables. Then I saw a chapter called "Bums in the Attic."

Passing bums will ask, Can I come in? I'll offer them the attic, ask them to stay . . .

My head buzzed. Even though Hannah hadn't read this in class, I heard her voice saying the words, and I felt sick and angry. I wanted to throw the book at the wall.

Maybe I was mad about the truck in the driveway or that they made my mom wait so long for the interview or the waving lady's face. Or maybe it was seeing Tom Bender's house. Or maybe I was mad because there was no way I could be somebody other than the dummy my parents made me.

I walked between the stacks, trying not to think at all, then because I might need to read it again, I reshelved the book exactly where it didn't belong. People usually look for things at eye level, did you ever notice that? Like Mr. Bender looking across the street and not seeing me. If you're not where they expect you, they might not see you. I buried the book on a bottom shelf.

A man laughed. I turned. Decorations were half-up, half-down. Pumpkin lights dangling to the floor, Pilgrim cutouts and paper turkeys waiting in the wings. I couldn't tell what was going up, what coming down. Had Halloween already come and gone? It was still on its way, wasn't it? When? What day was this?

A yellow aluminum ladder stood at one end of the reference desk, with a couple of open-flapped cartons on the floor next to it. A high school kid was up the ladder, reaching behind the INFORMATION sign over the desk to string up a coil of gold twinkly lights, while another intern fed the lights to him yard by yard. The librarians were joking with the interns, while the only man on the actual staff under age eighty held the ladder steady, a single foot planted on the bottom rung, showing off. All this was fine. Great. Stupid. Life doing what it's supposed to.

I was worming my way back to collect my stuff when I saw a copy of *Mango* on a study table with a binder and a water bottle. It wasn't the version Mr. M had given us in class, but older, with a hard cover. No one was sitting there, so I leaned against the table edge, picked it up, and looked inside. No underlining, no notes, but stars and dashes penciled up and down the margins.

"Hey."

I remembered that little girl on the "private court" in New Hampshire. I turned, ready. Hannah stood a few feet away, taller than me. Brown eyes, hair rusty brown and unbraided and wild, different from how she had it in class.

"Sorry," I said. "I was just..."

"Don't you love that book?"

I thought about that. "Probably not as much as you, but yeah. I haven't finished it, though. I lost my copy."

"They must have one here."

"All out, I checked."

Except why did I lie about that? She already had her own, so she wouldn't go hunting for the one I'd hidden. I don't know.

"Do you come here?" she asked. "I study here a lot. It's quiet and, well..." She waved her hand at the stacks as if to say, *Books!*

I shook my head. "Sometimes. Plus, my mother works across the street. Office manager." Why couldn't I tell her the truth? Why was everything a lie? Because it was easier? Distract them. Make them look away. Fade off.

I smelled myself and stepped back.

She sat down. "You should finish it. Really. The best part is the end. I first read it in sixth grade. This is my mom's book. Well, not *in* sixth grade. During the summer. This time was so much better. I saw so much more. I want to be her."

She was talking so fast.

"You want to be your mom?" I asked.

"No. She died when I was born. Well, just after."

"Oh, sorry. That's tough."

"Sometimes. But I mean I want to be her, Esperanza. But not her either. I want to be the author, who actually did get away and wrote all about it."

"So you think the book is true? It really happened?"

"True? Well, it's fiction...but it's sort of the author's story. I think so."

"Sort of. A metaphor, you said. But I get it." I didn't, but she was looking at me for more, so I added, "You sounded like a teacher in class. You could teach Mr. Maroni."

She laughed. It was the first time I'd heard her laugh and it sounded like bells. Dumb, but that's what it sounded like in the quiet library. Then she handed me the book, open at the end, shut her eyes, and quoted the whole last chapter from memory, from *I like to tell stories* to *For the ones who cannot out.* Of course she got it perfect, every sentence, every word. But it wasn't even that. It was as if

132

she was a singer and had just sung a song. Or recited a poem or a gospel, quietly and only to me. Secretly.

Then there was a moment.

When she stopped speaking but her eyes were still closed, her face went smooth from her forehead to her eyelids to her cheeks to her lips and chin. In that split second, I felt like leaning in and putting my cheek against her cheek, because I knew it would be warm. I don't know. I really did think that, but it was so wrong. Totally off base. But I thought it, so shoot me. Then it was past and she popped her eyes open.

"How did I do?"

"Yeah. You got it right. I have to find a copy."

"Well, you can't have mine," she said, collecting her stuff together in a big bag. "It's got all my mom's junk in it, her dashes. All my junk, too. I'm the stars. You gotta make your own junk." She laughed like bells again, then whisper-shouted, "Make your own junk!" But nobody looked.

She took a long breath, pulled her forest of hair back, let it go, and said, "I have to get moving, so I guess, you know, see ya."

I stepped back again. "Yeah. See you."

CHAPTER 23
HOPES

When ten minutes later I crossed the street to the office where Mom was, I was still thinking about Hannah. What's going on here? Her face, her voice, still working on me. I could have kept them inside for a long while, but I didn't have time, I didn't have space. Mom was done with her interview and standing there, smiling stiffly.

Before I said a word, she pulled me through the lobby to the parking lot.

"How did it go?" I asked when she beeped open the car.

"We'll know in a week or ten days."

"Ten days? We have to leave a week from Saturday."

We drove out the lot toward home.

"You never mind about that. I have hopes. I think they liked me. Everything they want this person to do is everything I can do. I've done it all. And more. I feel good about it, Jeff. Really good."

I hoped she was telling the truth. A new job might get Mr. Andrade and the marshal to back down. Then the usual thought crept in. That Mom had gotten it wrong, that they make everybody feel good after an interview and were just lying to her, humoring her until they hired someone else.

"Did they ask about getting fired from the clinic and the other job the clinic offered you?"

"A little. I got past it." She slowed for a stoplight but it turned green.

"Did the lady have a file or anything?" I said.

"A file?"

"You know. A report card. Like they had at the unemployment place."

"No. She might check, but I really didn't burn any bridges when I left those places. I was mad, but anybody would have been. I didn't make a scene."

I wondered if that was true. "Well, good. Perfect. Does that mean, if you get this job, that we can stay in our house?"

She half nodded. "The notice the sheriff gave me..."

"Marshal," I said, as we turned the corner onto our street.

"...I'll get a lawyer to get me an extension. If I can find one who won't chisel me. Anyway, I really feel good about the way this interview—"

She gulped back what she was going to say. A small

pickup and a van were parked at the house, the truck in our driveway, the van out front. The pickup must have been Mr. Andrade's.

"What the—" She pulled up short at the curb. "He's at it again!" She tore out of the car, leaving her door open, and started yelling at Mr. Andrade between her teeth.

"You said this wouldn't happen. You promised! What are you doing here? My house is my house until it isn't! You said. You said—"

"No, no, just painters. I am sorry, miss. Just seeing what needs to be done. I had to double-check how much paint. It's chilly in there. You should turn the heat up. You have a lot to do inside, yes?"

"You never mind what's inside!" she snapped. "I'll take care of it. Don't you worry."

I didn't know what to say. "Mom? The lawyer, tell him—"

She elbowed me to keep quiet.

"So, okay, okay," Mr. Andrade said, and got into his truck, while the other man, in painting overalls, came over. He slipped two fingers into a pocket and tweezered out a card. He held it to Mom.

"In case your new place needs any—"

The look she gave him. As if he were handing her a poop.

I took the business card. "Thanks."

He shrugged at me like, *What's with her?* and got into his van and left.

CHAPTER 24
GETTING COLDER

It was because I forgot to think.

It was because I believed my mother when she said she was taking care of us. It was because after Mom celebrated with her old nurse buddies last night about the interview—the interview!—she did her usual thing and fell asleep on the couch like all the other times.

We woke late on Sunday to pounding on the front door. I think I screamed. My first, crazy thought was that Hannah was mad because I stole what she said for our essay test last week. But no. From my window I saw Mr. Andrade. He was dressed in church clothes, his face red, looking in and pounding for a long minute, then jumping back down the steps to the marshal, whose car blocked our driveway.

We got to the door and opened it just as a moving van was rolling slowly to the curb. The sky was dark, gray with clouds.

"Oh, my lord!" my mother screamed. "No—"

"The oil com-company!" Mr. Andrade sputtered. "The oil company called me. Emergency. You didn't pay last two months. They didn't deliver. My furnace!"

"What?" Mom squeaked. "The liars! What?"

The cold water, the chilly mornings and nights. It was because I didn't think.

"Sludge in the pipes," Mr. Andrade went on. "The furnace sucks in all the dirty sludge if the tank is empty. They have to—probably have to drain the lines. New filters. My furnace!"

Mom just stood there shaking.

"You're leaving today," the marshal called out.

"We still have more time!" I said. "You said two weeks. It's not—"

"Time's up now," the marshal said, pushing himself away from his car, a different one from the car he had a week ago. "This house is unsafe. No heat, no hot water, no sir. We need to get you out. You have damaged the furnace, maybe thousands in costs, and it's not safe to live here. So...time's up." He worked his way up the walk side by side with the landlord, whose face was purple. "Tell us, ma'am. How can we help?"

Mom's shoulders shook and shook and wouldn't stop.

"There are services," the marshal said. "Rapid rehousing programs, you know. Shelters. In a pinch, the rescue mission downtown is where I'd go—"

"I don't want services. We don't need *services*!" she said. "I'm not...a bum."

"Except it happens a thousand times," he said. "What do you think I mostly do? I mostly do this. I see it. It's happening. Five, six streets up, Calder Lane? It's happening there, too. I can't say who, but heck, you might even know them—"

"I don't know them," she said.

"The point is," he said, "take what you need for a few days and put the rest in storage. You have storage? We have a van here, compliments of Mr. Andrade. It's not cheap, you know. And on a Sunday. You have storage? You said you would."

"Yes. I do."

"Good. Because Mr. Andrade went and hired this moving van just for you."

"You just said that," I said.

"On his dime," the marshal continued, ignoring me. "You don't have to pay for it, he did. You just tell his men where to take your things. You have enough storage? Did you rent enough space...?"

"She told you she did!" I said.

"All right. Just saying—"

"Can we have some privacy, please?" Mom said, grabbing at the door and stepping back in.

Mr. Andrade shot an angry look at the marshal,

chewed his lips for some very long seconds, then shrugged. "Half hour. We wait right here for you."

"One hour," said the marshal. "And yes, we'll wait."

Mom pulled me back in and closed the door on them, not bothering to flip the bolt, which I guess we both knew meant nothing anymore.

"Get your stuff. Just enough for a few days. Only what you absolutely need. We'll store the rest and get it back soon. I can't stay here anymore. People traipsing through. His stinking furnace. This isn't our home. It's just a cold house. Just rooms..."

"Grandpa's room."

"Never mind, honey. I...I'll figure something out. This is too horrible now. Don't worry, Jeff. Go on. Go on."

I should have realized it was coming, but I didn't. When I stumbled into my room I felt I was someone else, somebody I didn't know. My blood was ice. Like I'd just been killed but didn't know it yet. My body was still working, but it didn't have any life. I looked around at my stuff. Blurry. Meaningless. I wondered whose it was. We'd been selling things off, but I actually never thought about grabbing the stuff I'd need—*need*—to take with me. I hated that Mom hadn't done anything, or enough, to stop this, but there she was, cursing like crazy from the kitchen, and that brought me out of it.

My stuff, my things.

If you've ever been in a fire, I guess you'd know. Your

mind sputters when you have to run and grab and save stuff and mine was sputtering now.

Starving all of a sudden, I went to the kitchen. Mom had moved to her room. There was a black banana in a bowl. Glasses in the sink. Cloth shopping bags bulged on the counter under half-empty open cabinets. Grandpa put those cabinets up. His invisible fingerprints on them. The cabinets weren't ours anymore. The rooms weren't ours.

Sorry, Jeffie.

His voice moved in my mind and I could almost smell the pee in his little old room. His shrunken body, his single leg propped like a bone on the pillow. A stack of cartons now stood where his bed used to be, along with a couple sticks of furniture she hadn't sold.

I remembered the week after Grandpa died, Mom and me rolling up his old shirts and jackets and pants into garbage bags and putting them in her trunk for Goodwill. I don't know where my father was at the time. He didn't help us. He was out. I guess that was the start of it. Dad said Mom got bad for the first time after Grandpa died.

All downhill from there.

I was swimming, I couldn't focus.

Mom dragged suitcases noisily across the floor of her room, while I forced myself to grab idiotic junk. I was blind with the buzzing in my ears. I couldn't see or hear. When I opened my rolling bag it was still half full with what I didn't use on our stunted weekend in New Hampshire. Now I added what I really needed.

Black T-shirts, right? No matter how filthy you get, dirt doesn't show up on black. I tossed those in. Underwear, all I had. I scooped a handful of old comics from the floor next to my bed. My nightstand had gone last week.

Opening my dresser, I grabbed two pairs of chunky socks from my drawer. I usually wear the same pair for two weeks before my mother steals them for washing and forces me to break in a new pair. With two fresh pairs, I was good for a month. A month where? I had no idea. I spotted a tube of toothpaste and threw it in.

What else? The posters? My pillow? What a joke.

I may as well have put a bathmat in there, or a stapler, or a Christmas ornament, or the purple glove rolled up on the floor under my bed. Where was the other one? I didn't know what I was doing, wandering around my ex-house looking for what I used to be. I was this far from cracking the toilet bowl as a message, but I figured the marshal wouldn't like it and we'd have to pay for it with money we obviously didn't have.

"I'm all set," I said, rolling my dumb bag into Mom's room.

She was frozen at the edge of her bed, her cheeks shaking as she looked up at me. "I'm forty-three years old. How is it possible that this can happen to us?"

I looked around at the piles she'd started to make. Sweaters, shoes, underwear. It turned my stomach.

"Mom, we're running out of time...."

"I'll tell you how this happens," she said. "You marry a creep and he gives you a kid and he leaves and you think you were never good enough in the first place, but now you have a kid to take care of, and they throw you out of work and out of your house because of...because of what? Who did this to us?"

"Mom, we don't have time."

When I pushed her shoes off the bed into an open carton, she wailed and kicked the box over. The shoes tumbled out. The doorbell rang and the front door opened.

"Wake up, Mom," I said, and rolled my bag out.

Mr. Andrade stood in the doorway not speaking, his face not purple anymore. I could tell from the way his shoulders slumped that he was miserable and sorry he had to do this. Mom was out of her room now, her hands over her mouth, sobbing. Before I could do anything, she dropped to her knees in front of him.

"Mom!" I tried to pick her up, but she blubbered that we needed more time, more time, just a little more time.

The landlord bit his lip and let his cheeks go loose. Was he thinking about it? Considering it? Would he decide at the last minute that we could stay?

No.

"I'm showing the house tomorrow. Three appointments. Sorry. It has to be empty. I need your key. And the furnace isn't working. And maybe something else needs to be fixed...."

I wanted to punch something, scream and punch and punch, but I had to answer for my mom, because all she was doing was crying. "We know," I said. "We're nearly ready."

The door opened again, no bell this time, no knock. The marshal's big shape hovered in the door frame like in every bad movie.

"Sorry, but it's time to wrap this up," he said, checking his watch, then sliding aside like he was in the room of a dying person he barely knew. I wondered how many times he really had played this part. The policewoman stood behind him now, the same one as before. She put on a tight smile, came in, and helped my mom up from the floor. She then handed Mom a big envelope.

"There are offices in downtown Bridgeport that will help if you need help finding a place to stay tonight," she said. "Really, the people are great there. Call two-one-one, Emergency Services, they'll get you started and tell you where to get assistance. And it's getting colder, so you should check them out."

"Colder?" I said. "What does that have to do with anything?"

My mother took the envelope and whispered, "Downtown Bridgeport," but I didn't know what she meant. What about downtown Bridgeport?

"Would you like me to call a shelter for you now?" the policewoman offered. "I can do that for tonight. There are lawyers, too. Twenty-four hour hotlines, if you want."

"No, th-thanks, thank you." Mom pushed out the front door for probably the last time. "Not tonight. We have a place tonight. We're fine tonight."

Which was the second scariest thing she could have said.

What about tomorrow night? And the night after that?

I thought of my month's worth of socks. My mind spun and spun.

Like they were frozen where they stood, everyone watched me drag our boxes out and lift them into the trunk of our car. Then I stuffed our rolling bags and groceries into the backseat.

The worst part came after Mom gave the movers the address of the storage facility and the two of us were huddled on the sidewalk together. As we watched them take stuff, wrap it, and stow it deep in the van, Mom all at once ran back, gave Mr. Andrade the single house key, then took his hand and held it tight between hers.

"Please, my mail. I beg you. Leave it in the box for me, yes? If anybody asks, we're still here, okay? We're still here for I don't know how long, but a couple of weeks at least? Okay? I need that. I need an address to tell people. Please."

She was out of control and shaking like a sick person.

"I'm not hearing this," the marshal said, turning away. "Your decision, sir."

The landlord nodded slowly and said, "Sure, sure. Whatever you need. As long as I can. I'm sorry, but five months no rent, damage, you understand. I have no choice. My wife had surgery."

Which shook Mom. She didn't know. Maybe she didn't care. There were more words from him and the policewoman, about things that might help. Even the marshal pitched in some ideas, but that was all I heard. The noise in my head was deafening.

———

We got in the car and drove around the streets until she saw a CVS. She pulled into the parking lot and searched her phone for hotels and motels and called five or six before one said they had a room at a good price. "Finally," she said with a snort. "And it's not far."

"Does it have a pool?" I asked. "Indoor. Mom. Pool. Need. Me."

"Jeff! You...don't joke, honey, don't."

"At least a Jacuzzi, then. Or am I thinking of Zamboni? Or is Zamboni a kind of pasta? I get confused, don't you?"

She turned her red face to me. "You're a Zamboni." She wiped her cheeks. "You make everything better. Come on. The Sidespot Inn. Sounds cozy, huh? You and me?"

My head screamed. I swallowed my words and couldn't speak until she started the car and pulled back into traffic.

"Yeah," I said. "Yeah, it does."

CHAPTER 25
THE SIDESPOT INN

The Sidespot Inn *wasn't*.

It was the Sidespot *Motor* Inn, which is a different deal altogether, and it was practically *on* the exit ramp right off the interstate in the middle of Bridgeport. We missed it the first time, because the sign was so bad it only said DESPO in big letters and OTOR I in little ones, so we had to take the turnpike back an exit and try again.

"Yay, we made it," I said when we pulled into the lot.

"This isn't what I had in mind," Mom said. "The website sounded better."

"That's why they invented websites. To fool people."

Which I thought was smart and a little funny, but she didn't.

We idled for a few minutes in the shadows and since shadows were pretty much everywhere under the highway, it was hard not to be in them. My brain was shooting sparks while Mom was deciding whether to stay or go.

We needed a joke, so I said, "Maybe they meant to call it Side*stop*, because you *stop* on the *side* of the highway. And *Motor Inn* because you just *motor in* right from the ramp. Am I right?"

She was silent as death and far from laughing. Groaning what sounded like her last breath, she puttered the car over to the entrance and parked outside the lobby, where tall glass windows spilled yellow light from inside.

"Looks okay. For a night. Or two." I threw that out there to see what she'd say.

She puffed out a single word. "Until..."

But she didn't go anywhere with it, so I had to finish for her.

"Until we get this sorted out?"

"That."

Honestly, I didn't know how she'd sort it out. We were out of our house, it was getting colder by the minute, Mom was a wreck, we had only the barest stuff—the craziest junk, those socks!—and it was a school day tomorrow. I felt my stomach drain into my legs.

A buzzer rang when we entered the office, dragging our bags over a rug where someone had died. The stain was the shape of a body dropped from high overhead. Unmatched floor lamps stood on either side of a short couch across from a counter paneled with brown paneling and that had a green-shaded lamp and a blotter on top. A man came out from a room behind the counter and didn't smile. Gray hair. Stubble. Wrinkles under his eyes like one of those wrinkly dogs. Smoke whirled in with him as if from the gate of hell. I'm pretty sure it was cigarette smoke.

"Mmm?" he grumbled, which seemed a big deal from him.

Mom gave him a flat smile. "I called. Earlier. Forty-nine dollars a night, you said."

"Mmm," he said again, then nodded his chin at me. "Just so you know, it's five extra for a cot. You want a cot?"

Mom searched my face. I don't know what she was hoping to get from me. Did she want me to sleep on the floor? Was she going to give me the bed and sleep on the floor herself? For five lousy dollars?

"Yes, a cot," I said, and he bent his eyes below the counter where his hands were rustling. He came up with a card the exact size of a large index card, because it was a large index card.

"Name and address here, phone number, make and model of car. No parties after school, just so you know." He was half looking at me when he said this.

I felt like saying, *Who would have a party* here? Instead, I said, "I'm not a party person, really."

"Just so you know." Which, along with "Mmm," was his favorite phrase.

She wrote on the card. With a single finger, he spun it

around on the counter and frowned. "So, why you staying here if you live right there?"

She said "Remodeling" and I said "Fumigating" at the same time.

He snorted a wet laugh. "Whatever. Two keys?"

"Thank you," she said.

He totaled up the amount and she counted out cash, when I suddenly thought of something. "Is there any discount by the week?"

He raised an eyebrow. "Mmm?"

Mom frowned but said nothing, which made me think a week was possible. At least it would take the pressure off, right? The man tugged a calculator from the mess under the counter and tapped in numbers. "If we do night by night, a week comes to three-ninety-seven, including tax. I can let you have it for three-fifty, the week. I'll upgrade you to a suite and knock off part of the cot, too. Three-twenty. Half in advance. How's that? Includes tax. Mmm?"

He was being more open now, not so grumpy. It must have been the thought of all those possible dollars at once. Mom eyed me, again looking for I don't know what, then put away her cash and took out a credit card. "Will this work...?"

"Let's find out," he said.

I knew she wasn't sure if the card would go through, but he ran it and it did. She signed the receipt, and he gave us two keycards for the room.

Suite 214 was on the upstairs level. A girl passed us going down while we climbed the stairs. It wasn't Hannah, of course, but I thought about her. I thought about Hannah a lot, I don't know why. The railing overlooked the parking lot. Our car was nearly alone down there. There were six others spread around the lot. When we opened the room door Mom arched back from the smell that came out, which was like bowling shoes. The *suite* was a single room and it was small and the carpet was thin and worn and stained from liquids spilled on it, but a light by the bed was on, and the room was warm.

"Big bed," I said.

"It's a queen. Queen size."

"Of course," I said. "They knew you were coming."

I thought: I really am funny. But I guess the words came out snippy because she bit her lips tight, didn't look at me.

"I'll call a few friends in the morning," she said.

"Hey, no parties," I said, so nervous I couldn't stop myself.

"For ideas about where to stay. There has to be something better. Maybe we'll only stay the half week we paid for. We'll see."

To fill up the sad air, I said, "Sounds good," and wheeled my bag in. She pulled hers to the dresser. She didn't open it, but sat on the edge of the bed.

"It's okay, right?" I said. "I mean, it's not that bad."

"It's a place. But then what, Jeff? Tell me that. A week here, then what?"

"I don't know," I said. "For crying out loud, Mom— how should I know? I'm not the genius around here. I mean, I am, but still—"

"All right, all right, never mind. Bolt the door, will you, honey?"

Before I could do that the manager appeared, wheeling a squeaky cot along the landing. He rolled it past me into the room, when I saw not-Hannah leaning against a car in the lot below our room, smoking.

Mom didn't get up from the bed.

"Where?" he said.

"Here." I helped him steer the cot into the only available place, which was outside the bathroom and in front of the TV. "Thanks."

"It's already made up. Don't scratch the walls with it, just so you know."

"Got it," I said.

"Night, then." He turned and left the room, closing the door softly behind him.

I bolted the door. Mom was still sitting on the edge of the bed, which had sunk down under her weight. I unlocked the cot and tried to hold the two halves of the frame upright, but the head slipped, hit the wall, and ran down it before I could pull it away. There was a neat line through the paint.

"Just what he told me not to do!" I almost laughed.

Mom looked at me, then at the scratch, and shrugged. "You never liked people giving you orders."

"I know, right?" I dug into my bag, then stopped short. "Dang. I totally forgot my trunks!"

She slowly unzipped her own bag. "Because you're a Zamboni."

CHAPTER 26
BEAUTIFUL MORNING

It was dark as a coffin when I woke.

Where was I? My mother snored in my left ear. Oh. The room. The motel. The motor inn. I couldn't tell what direction I was facing. Black air all around.

What time was it? What time *of day* was it?

Clawing at the nightstand between us for her phone: 5:52 AM blazed white in my face. Bare feet on the thin cold carpet. Trying not to smash my toes into anything. I finally found the window and cracked open the heavy curtains.

A universe of fog.

The glow from the highway was sick yellow. Headlights were dull spots, like flashlights with dying batteries. The morning rush of traffic made no sound.

My new world.

I opened the room door and breathed in cold and exhaust. A second sniff gave me a nearby bakery and the odor of cigarette smoke. I thought of that girl smoking in the lot last night. That led me to Hannah and her face. Why do I think about girls so much? Rich's dirty remark came into my head. I couldn't even go there. School and classes and books and friends and even girls seemed stupid and pointless.

I closed the door. I couldn't stomach all the trouble of getting wet in the shower, then all the drying. Sniffing the armpits of the T-shirt I'd worn yesterday, I figured another day wouldn't kill me. Or anyone else, if I kept my distance. Jeans, of course, only changing my underwear, which I dug out of my bag. I put on my first fresh pair of socks, starting a two-week run in them. Washed my face. Warm water. Brushed my teeth. But why? The thought of walking into school like this seemed the dumbest idea in the world. From my house to school is one thing, but from a skeevy smelly motel to a classroom full of normal kids?

By the time I flicked off the bathroom light, Mom's foot was out of the covers. I didn't want to look at it. Grandpa's cold white single dying foot. But I had to wake her.

I jerked my knee into her mattress. "Mom?"

A snort of air. "What? What?"

"Time to get up."

"What? Okay—" She hit her elbow on the nightstand and cursed.

"Keep it down," I said. "You'll wake the neighbors."

I thought it might sound funny, like a parent scolding a child, but it wasn't funny, not even to me. My chest ached. Had I become the grown-up? Standing there fully dressed and waiting while Mom blinked herself awake?

I felt cold and alone and couldn't stop my tongue.

"You know, I knew this was going to happen. I saw the whole thing coming."

"Jeff, what? What happened?"

"Us. This. I knew we'd come here after Dad left. This is where we'd be. Eventually. And here we are. I knew it would turn out this way."

It felt as if someone else were saying those words, forcing them out my mouth, not me. Except it *was* me. I was saying this because I believed it.

"You did not know it." She sat up in bed now, her pajamas sliding off her shoulder.

I turned away so I wouldn't see. "Except I did. I do. I've been waiting for us to crash every day since he ran out. Now we have."

She stood up, fixed her top, and faced me. "Since he left?" She coughed a dismissive breath. "Him? We made our own lives since he left, you and me. We don't need him. We're making it up ourselves, and we're okay. I'm telling you, Jeffie, we're okay. This is just a little..."

Don't say *bump*!

"...a little bump, that's all. We don't need him, and all his old rubbish and younger women and lies and no money, forget him."

"Except if we're making it all up, why isn't it better? What do we do now? What's the next thing? You said you'd call friends—"

"I will. Today."

"Why not skip that and go straight into the system?"

"Don't ever say that! Never. Never, Jeff." She came across the floor and put her arms around me. "That will never happen. You will not, and I will not. Jeff, never."

I wondered how long until *never* would happen. Weeks? Days?

Stepping back, she searched my face. I don't think she saw much in the dim light of the parted curtains. She cleared her throat.

"What do we do now? Ha. I'll tell you what we do now, mister. *You* go down and bring us back some bagels and coffee from the lobby, while *I* get in the shower. Get some java for yourself, if you need it. *That's* what we do now!"

She'd taken over sounding grown-up now. She had to sometime. Her day was...how horrible *was* her day going to be? Calling friends, asking them for money or a couch to sleep on, not just for her, but for her son, too? How humiliating is that?

All I had to do was sit at a desk all day and try to stay awake. She had to fall on her knees in front of everyone, stroke their hands, and beg.

So I said, "Okay, Mom. Breakfast coming up," and I said it as perkily as I could.

CHAPTER 27

THE FACE OF JESUS

School was, I can't even tell you. I'm not sure I understood a word of anything anyone said. After Mom picked me up we drove to where she'd rented two storage pods—the first month free, she told me. They weren't far from the Sidespot. Our stuff was jammed in like you wouldn't believe.

"Movers!" she said. "Like animals."

Tables piled on tables, chairs to the ceiling, cartons upon cartons, trash bags of clothes pushed into every space in between. It started to avalanche when I tried to ease a bag out, so I left it.

Mom rummaged for a purse she was sure had cash, and she found it. "Twenty-two dollars!" she crowed. My eyes stung. I turned away and dug into a carton marked *Jeff,* hoping to find the missing book. There were a couple of others, but not *Mango.* I had to face it. It was under a bed in a pink cottage on a lake two hundred miles from here.

"You're not going to start reading now," she said, not expecting an answer.

I tried to remember the look of Hannah's mother's copy, her stars penciled in the margins of the pages, but it wasn't coming. Among the junk from my desk drawers was the holy card I'd found last year, the one with the face of Jesus on one side and a photo of my grandfather on the other. The photo was taken the year before he died. He had longish hair, greasy and dark. His face was thin. There was a shadow of stubble on his cheeks. His eyes were pockets, gray-brown and glassy as he looked into the camera. Behind him you could see the hazy shape of an old steam locomotive. He was already so sick and sad and missing a leg, but he wanted to show me train stuff. I was four and I remember he had his hand on my shoulder and I was smiling, but I was cropped out for the holy card. I slipped it into my pocket, thinking of him and of Mom, who was scrounging for more money, and for some reason I thought of Hannah, too, and I felt everything sink inside me.

It's weird that the moment you name it—being poor—it goes from being a bunch of blurry forms hovering around you like ghosts to a solid thing with arms and hands and a face and strength and hate. And the thing it hates is you, because the instant you give it a name, it knows you well enough to want you dead.

———

The days went on.

I tried to tell Mom no one knew or really cared, but she was so paranoid for school not to think anything weird was going on with us, she was careful to drop me at school and pick me up on time, all smiles. On days when I took the bus to my old stop I hung in our backyard until she beeped from the street, which was an okay system, unless it rained.

Trucks were there nearly every day doing repairs. I wondered what it was looking like inside now, but I never went in. Warmer probably. They didn't want the new pipes glopping up with old oil. There'd be saws and sanders and smooth new wood everywhere, which reminded me of Grandpa. The mail was always in the box, a lot of junk mail, but it was all there. Mr. Andrade was good about that, at least.

Except not "at least." He didn't owe us anything. We owed him. Seven thousand dollars. Plus repairs. We were the thieves.

When Mom was busy until suppertime, I waited at the library, a twenty-five-minute walk from our old house. My bike would have been good for getting around, and Mr. Andrade would probably have let me keep it in the shed. I could hear him saying it was fine. But we'd sold the bike early on for, amazingly, more money than for the love seat and chairs put together, because she went to an actual bike shop to sell it.

"There's a big business in used bikes, kid," the creep had said when he wheeled my Mongoose into the back of his shop.

I felt then like that kid who had to leave Winnie-the-Pooh behind and grow up.

I was heading to the library one afternoon, some afternoon, Thursday of our first motel week, maybe. The day before, I'd discovered the book was no longer where I'd hidden it. Maybe someone checked it out or maybe the staff tossed it because it was beat up. I hoped Hannah was there, so I might read hers, when I found myself slowing down at the corner of Gresham Road. Among the trees at the end was a church steeple.

St. Catherine's.

It wasn't that late. Mrs. Tracy might still be there. The hill blocked the sun. The air was crackly and cold. The cop lady had said, *It's getting colder,* and I hadn't understood what she meant. Well, this was what she meant. Walking around without a home to go to, lurking in backyards when it gets cold. It's different from when it's sunny and the days are long. Cold tires your muscles, your face. Cold makes everything harder.

I pulled open the school doors. The halls breathed their old smell on me. A lone secretary in the office talked on the phone while flapping sheets of pink paper. I slipped up the stairs and searched for Mrs. Tracy's new room in the eighth-grade wing. I saw her name over the last one on the left. I peeked in. The front lights were on, but the room was empty. I imagined her face, but it faded quickly. I searched the shelves under the window. The book wasn't there. Of course. It wouldn't be a book they'd read at Catholic school.

I sat at the desk at the head of the second row, where I'd sat last year. A fleck of white drifted outside the window. I remember I used to look at the woods a lot. Now, deep in the afternoon, the sky was very low. Wind was moving the high branches, bare and gray. Another flake. Colder. It was getting colder. The policewoman's face again.

There was the past and there was now and I felt the room come down on me. My heart thudded, my vision tunneled. My face and head itched all over. I swallowed hard, trying not to let it happen. I needed to leave the classroom before I started to cry.

The hallway was dead empty when I went out. The secretary's office was dark.

I pushed out the front doors and found Courtney Zisky and her long hair standing on the sidewalk by the flagpole.

CHAPTER 28
ALL OF THEM

She did a double take when she heard the school doors suck open—seeing me, turning away, then turning back. It was comical, except for her face.

"Jeff?" she said. "What are you doing here?"

Courtney was as good-looking as last year. Better. Taller, her hair longer, her cheeks pink from the cold. Her coat was wrapped tight. I don't know if she wore a sweater. I almost wasn't going to tell you that I wondered about that, but why not?

I didn't want to talk. To anybody, especially not her, and I was mad that she'd seen me, so it came out angry. "Why do you care?"

She jerked her head sharply. "What?"

And in that word, that one word, it was like she was so disgusted she couldn't believe it. Like she was a person and I was slime. My stomach wrung tight and all my old angry feeling came back. I felt humiliated with Mom, but I'm pretty sure she thought I was worth something.

"Don't worry," I said. "I won't darken your towels again."

Which probably confused her, but is a line from a Marx Brothers movie.

"Same old Jeff." She smirked. "I don't know what in the world you're saying."

"Yeah, well, you never liked me."

She screwed up her face like she smelled my socks. "I never *not* liked you."

"You didn't think twice about me, all the same. Even though . . . even though I voted for you, for class president last year." My breath left me. "Just never mind."

"Hey, you don't get to say that. And why should I think *anything* about you, Jeff? You were snotty in class. To Mrs. Tracy. To other people. You were plain mean to some of us. You know who I'm talking about."

All of a sudden Jessica Feeney was in my head, her scars, her melted hands. Except she wasn't even the thing. It was that Tom was the only person—the only smart person—who ever gave a rat about me, but after Jessica he made every excuse not to hang out.

No surprise there, right? I get to be too much myself, too comfortable, say what's in my head, and everyone gets weird. That's what I do. I make good things turn the other way. All anyone saw was that I didn't want to hold her burned hand and all I know is that being me wasn't good enough anymore.

I stared at Courtney, feeling myself drain away to nothing. "Blah-blah-blah."

"People see things, Jeff, and they can't figure out why you do and say what you do. I know I can't."

"So you *do* think about me." I grinned like some kind of dirty old man.

"Right, because that's the point of all this. You're so full of yourself and think you know things, but you aren't as funny as you think you are. Go home."

It was like she was smacking me left and right. *Full of myself?* Ha! I was full of nothing. And *home?* There I was in the parking lot at St. Catherine's, looking down the sidewalk at some street, and I totally blanked on where I was supposed to go next. This way, that way? Where do I live? That's funny, isn't it? Somebody says *Go home,* but you don't have one.

"Jeff?"

I spun around. Tom Bender was leaning oddly a few steps off, his pants flapping in the wind like always, last year's blazer short at the cuffs. He might have been taller and thinner, but his face was the same, with his dumb look of half worry, half surprise.

"So..." he said, his eyes, like always, waiting for something.

Every terrible thing that happened between us last

year surged up in me, and I started yelling. Not the string of cursing you might think. Just one long animal scream.

"Ahhhhhh!"

I ran, stumbling down the sidewalk, tripping into someone's yard. My throat burned. I wanted to rip my clothes. I fell in the next yard, got up on my stick legs. I wanted to be home, bury myself in bed, pull a blanket over my head. But there was no home, no blanket, no bed of my own. Waves crashed and crashed on me, icing my spine all the way up. I fell again, got up, and ran.

What was I doing there? What did St. Catherine's mean to me anyway? I must have had a rotten time if the only person I came away with was Rich.

Why did I come back here?

To prove to myself that I don't belong?

CHAPTER 29
WE MOVE AGAIN

The next day, we got the bad news.

"I didn't get the job."

I sat in the front seat, sinking through the floor as she drove out of the library lot. Her breath filled the car. I was scared out of my head and angry, because I knew why she didn't get it, why she really lost the Fairchild Manor job, and the hospital job before that, knowing that this would be the way with all of them.

I wanted to ask, *Why do you drink in the afternoon, Mommy?* and she'd spit back, *What? No! Shut up. No, Jeffie, honey,* then get all teary, but I couldn't.

All that came out was a noise, a push of air up my throat.

"I know," she said. Her eyes were damp. "I was their second choice. They called. Out of fourteen applicants. That's good. It means if something opens up, they'll call me—"

"Did they say something would open up?"

"No. But if it does..."

I couldn't go there. "So. What's next? Anything? Or nothing."

She put her hand on my arm, giving it a little squeeze. "We tighten our belts a bit. The motel's letting us out of our week early, with a refund. It was nice but too pricey to keep going."

Was it? Was it nice?

"I was talking to Erin again today, and she said we could stay with her, at her house, for a short while."

"Erin? Who's Erin?"

"Erin Petry. From the hospital. You know."

I didn't. "Where does she live?"

"That's the great thing. On Birmingham Street in the north end. Just over the line."

I tried to picture her and the street. "How far from my school bus stop? Can I keep taking the same bus as for home?"

She looked at me the longest time, and I knew she was hoping I would lose that word, just banish the idea of *home* from my head. "Not far at all. Across Park Avenue. You can keep using the same bus stop."

"Uh-huh, okay. I guess. Okay."

———

After collecting our stuff from Stinkspot, we ate supper at Duchess and drove around until eight, then pulled up in front of a house seven short blocks from our old one and not as nice as it. A tall, thick woman came to the door when we got out of the car.

"Thank you so much for this, Erin," my mother said. "A night or two, until we get things straightened out." They did a cheek kiss in the doorway while I lugged the bags up the walk.

Until we get things straightened out. Why was it *we?* Did *I* get us here? Should I be doing more to get us back on track? Should I be doing all of it?

"Sure, honey. I'm sorry. Come on in, both of you."

"I'm Jeff, by the way," I said, moving past them.

"Of course, dear. I'm so sorry, but you'll both be comfy. What can I get you?"

"Nothing," I said. "Thanks."

I didn't catch her eye. You learn not to do that, make eye contact. I'm not great at it anyway, but I didn't even try now. Don't make contact, don't get close. I knew I was smelling more and more anyway, and smelling is a homeless thing.

Home. Homeless. Funny how it doesn't take much to go from one to the other.

Erin brought us upstairs. "I made up your beds," she said, two little kids tramping behind her as if they were leashed to her legs. Then we went up another set of stairs to a small room with sloped ceilings in front and back, two giant toy chests, and a dormer between two tiny beds.

"It's their playroom," she said, "but now it's just for you."

It was the attic. My throat fell into my stomach, fell into my legs, through the floors of the house and into the ground. You have to be kidding. She was putting us in the attic. Bums in the attic. She was hiding us like Dad wanted to hide Grandpa.

Erin smiled and backed out to the landing. "The bathroom is small, but it's all yours; we're on the floor below. Don't mind the toys. We'll make sure the boys stay out."

"Mom?" one boy said.

"Shh," said his brother. They looked like twins.

"Erin, thank you so much," Mom said. "You're a lifesaver."

Erin left with the twins. Mom carefully didn't look at me, just lowered her face, rolled her bag to the wall, and slowly unzipped it. She pulled out underwear or something and went off to the bathroom.

I shouldn't be sleeping in the same space as my mother. The hotel was bad enough, but together in the same room in someone's house? It was so wrong and weird. While she was in the bathroom, I flopped down on one of the beds, then tried the other, then went back to the first, which was better, then took the other one because Mom needed her sleep more than me. It was then I realized these were really kid beds.

"Seriously?" I said to the ceiling. "I hate my life!"

Nighttime was, no surprise, very special.

The junky bedsprings of my junky kid bed sagged in the middle and squeaked. I found by squeezing myself to the edge and hanging my arm over and not moving, I could actually doze off. The silver lining? It only took a half hour to get the feeling back in my hand.

All night long that first night I dreamed twenty-seven. Everything was twenty-seven. Somebody was announcing it or whispering it every few seconds. There were signs saying it, like highway signs. Chalk numbers on the sidewalk. Football jerseys.

When I woke up, I figured it out. Even without knowing I was doing it, I'd started counting days. It was twenty-seven days since Mom lost her job.

CHAPTER 30

GHOSTING

It went like that through a miserable rainy weekend and into the next week.

Tuesday was a skip-lunch day, but I sat with Colin and Josh because they saw me and it seemed odd not to. I spotted Hannah sitting on the far side of the cafeteria listening to a couple of other girls, back to her quiet self. She didn't notice me.

Colin dug into his mac and cheese and said, "Are you dying?"

"We all are," Josh said. "We started the day we were born. My rabbi said so."

"No, I meant you." Colin nodded his chin me. "You're always sneaking off, like my dog before he died. I'd find him hiding in the ivy. Plus you don't eat much when you are here. Two and two, you're dying."

"Can't argue with the math," said Josh, raising his hand for a high five, which Colin blew a kiss at, which

Josh pretended to eat, which Colin pretended to puke at, like they do it all the time.

"I'm in training," I said.

"For?"

"Getting older. School food will kill you."

"So have an apple," Josh said, then rolled his across the table at me. "Colin puts his fruit in bowls, but I hear you can eat these, too. Also they keep the doctor away."

"Doctor?" Colin raised his head. "Doctor who?"

"Doctor Fartface, aka, you."

Then, as if that skit was over, Colin said, "Tough test. *Mango*."

I bit into the apple and looked over at Hannah again. "I nearly flunked it."

"I'm sure *she* didn't," Colin said, seeing me look.

Josh gawked at her, too. "No, dang, she didn't, not with those amazing legs!"

"You and legs," Colin said.

"You and farts. You should know. You're the doctor of them!"

Like everything was a routine.

———

After school I holed up in the attic like a dying dog, until I suddenly remembered Rich Downing and figured I had to keep doing things with him or everybody would find out everything. Can't have that, can we?

In my brain I heard my mother snapping at me: *Why do you still think about those bums?* She was right. Not that they were bums, but why did I still care. I almost *didn't*, but I must have, a little.

I passed my old house on the way to Rich's. Trucks were in the driveway. Someone on the roof tapping at the chimney. I wanted to spit.

Rich blinked at me when he answered his door, like I'd just returned from the Arctic or somewhere. He came out on the step, letting the door close behind him.

"What's up?" he said.

"Next week is Thanksgiving," I said. "What presents do you think you'll get?"

He seemed bewildered. "Presents? Where have you been? I went by your house the other day. All the vans and trucks. What's going on?"

It was chilly on the step. We were usually inside by now. "That's for legal stuff." I blurted this out so easily I might have been practicing it. "The landlord gets to pay less taxes or something if he says the work's for a new rental rather than just remodeling it for the current people. The sign is just for show." Then I cupped my mouth and whispered. "He's secretly fixing it up for us!"

"Cool." He seemed to mean it. "When will you get back in? And where's all your stuff in the meantime? It looks empty."

"Storage. We're staying in Westport now. By the

water. There's a dock and a motorboat." This was all just spurting out of me but it sounded good.

"Westport? What about school?"

"What about it?"

"Well, you still go to Fairfield Plains, right? Can you live in Westport and go to school here? Don't you have to live here?"

A spear of panic hit my chest. "What? No. They said it's okay, the school people. It's just for a little while, anyway. So, you want to hang out for a couple of hours?"

He made a considering kind of face. "Nah. I have a big homework thing."

And just like that, I knew. The way he said it. *Nah.* I got it. I understood. Homework thing. Church thing. All the same.

I should have turned and just gone away, but where would I go? Back to the hidden attic? Another tired walk to the library? Rich wasn't the greatest, but outside Colin and Josh, who were practically strangers, he was the last one left.

And now he gives me *Nah*?

I decided to break it off. I was mad and I wanted to rip it to shreds.

"Homework, huh? I've heard that lie before. You think my mom is a drunk."

"What? No! And it's not your mom, anyway. It's mine. What she told me."

My throat tightened. They all sound alike when they lie to you. I half wanted to wipe the scared look off his face. Half wanted to scream because his mom was right.

"You know what, I don't even care."

"Hey, I stuck up for you," he said. "I told her your mother was just sad."

"Sad? What does that mean?"

"She said your mom drinks booze, booze, booze! I said I only saw it one time, and everybody drinks and they do, too. She got really mad and said we can't hang out."

Perfect. Everyone knows my mom drinks. There was no way out of this. I wasn't going to beg. He was right, his mother was right. At that instant, I drained myself more empty than I'd ever been. My eyes went out of focus. My blood stopped flowing. I turned and walked down the street toward my old house.

He might have said something, called me back, but probably not and I didn't hear him anyway. All it took was one word. *Nah.* And Rich faded like a ghost.

Good for him. He pulled a Mr. Andrade. A Courtney. A Tom Bender. I would have done the same thing. My mom and I were toxic and Rich finally realized it.

The last thread holding me down had been cut, and I understood that Rich wasn't the ghost, after all. I was.

CHAPTER 31
A MINUTE TO CALM DOWN

The next day I walked to the Petrys' house after another numb day at school. I wandered slowly from the bus stop, taking over an hour, nearly two, to wind through the streets, not that anyone cared. I had to empty my head of the shrieking. Of people, their faces, their voices, what they wanted from me. But I found it's hard to be clear of everything, because no matter how much you get rid of, *you're* always there, bringing yourself with you wherever you go, cluttering up your own space.

Yeah. Clutter. Thanks, Dad. I'm starting to get it.

It was nearly suppertime when I finally climbed the attic stairs and found my mother rocking on the edge of her bed. Her lips were as tight as if they'd been sewn together, and her cheeks were twitching like a bad reader.

She raised her face. I expected her to speak. She didn't.

"Mom? You're looking very weird. What's going on?"

She reached for my hand and sandwiched it between hers. "It's...it's time, Jeffie."

My veins froze. "For what? It's time for what? Mom?"

She gave me a dead smile, hoping I'd understand so she wouldn't have to say.

"Mom?"

Nothing. Just the face.

Sliding my hand out from hers, I tramped down the stairs and searched the rooms until I found odd little Ricky Petry alone in the kitchen.

"What happened?" I said to him. "Why is my mother a zombie? She's just sitting there in our room."

He backed away and had flattened his mouth as if to say, *I don't know!* when his mother came in.

"Oh, hi, Jeff, I am sorry," she started, but she must have figured from my face that I didn't know what was going on, because she said, "Oh, well, it's that you and your mom— it's time to think about finding a new place." She let that hang there for a bit, then added, "It's been a week, nearly a week, and now we really need you to move along."

"What happened?"

"Your mom can tell you."

"No, please. She's comatose. You tell me."

Erin breathed in. "She got a call today. Some job. But then she...well, let her tell you. Really, I'm sorry, Jeff. I'm sorry. For you, mostly—oh."

Mom was standing behind me, her face red. "Erin, please... you're our..."

Erin shook her head. "No, no, Michelle. It's only because you're a friend that...but look, stop doing this, what you're doing."

"It wasn't that bad."

I felt as clueless as weird little Ricky. "What are you two talking about?"

"It is, Michelle. It is that bad. We open our house to you, my husband, my children. You have everything here, and what you said to us? You should think about getting some help. Drink...less. This isn't working for you, or for your poor son. You know what I mean. Michelle, you know. I mean, look where you are...."

"What is going on?" I asked.

Mom was quiet for a long while. "Yes. I know. Of course, I know."

I was horrified for Mom. She was being humiliated by her "friend." I hated living with people. I tugged her out of the kitchen and back upstairs. I closed the attic door.

"Mom—"

"Jeff, it wasn't that bad. What I said. I was rude, but I was happy. They should have seen I was happy. I got the job. I think I got the job. A very good call this afternoon. They want to see me again. The other person's not working out. And I celebrated—"

"Celebrated? This afternoon? How could you do that? Never mind, I know how."

"I said things. About this. This room. This cramped little...hole. An *attic*, for heaven's sake! What *are* we? It wasn't nice, what I said. I wasn't very nice, but still..."

"Mom, you wrecked it for us? Again. I hate this dump, too, I hate it, but you're wrecking things more than I am!"

"Wrecking things? Jeff, no—"

"You know what, never mind. Never mind! What are we going to do now? Where do we go?"

"I understand you're angry, but Jeffie, I'm going to get this job. The office manager? I just feel it."

"You feel it."

"I think we need to feel good about that. This could be the turnaround we need."

"Turnaround. Mom, where do you get these things? Where do we go right now?"

Her dumb look again. Then her eyes grew super-huge and she bolted to her feet, nearly fell over, but righted herself with a hand on the dresser.

"Not here!" she shouted. "I can tell you that!"

"Well, yeah, but—"

"Shut—" She stopped, breathed. "Jeff, put your things together. Put them together right now. Not here. Not another word. Not another word in this awful house!"

It only took minutes and we were out in the car. No

words, her to me, or us to them. Words were done. The only hint of good-bye was the twins, staring at us from the front window with their mouths gaping at the freaks driving away.

She drove like a machine. No sound. No expression. Barely stopping at corners and lights, weaving and lurching. "Mom, are you okay? Pull over. You need to pull—"

She slammed on the brakes and swung her head at me. "What!"

It was hard looking at her face, red and hanging there. "You're scaring me," I said.

Someone honked behind us and she tore off down the street until she swerved into a parking lot, a big one, and kept on swerving, left and right, until she braked and hit a curb. She threw the car into park. There were cars near us, but not many. It didn't look like anyone had seen our jerky stop, and amazingly we were in an actual parking space.

"I... can't... see... what..." she mumbled.

I expected her to go on. "Mom?"

"I need to calm down. You'll let me do that, won't you, Jeff? Calm down? I need to calm down. I need..." She jerked her seat back, reclining it, then let out a long heavy breath. "Just give me a minute, just one minute!"

The parking lot lights had long ago flicked on. We sat there, the car running, the heat on, her head settled on the headrest. The fuel gauge said we were nearly empty.

It was dark, just before six. There were two big box stores in the lot. An office supply and a HomeGoods.

"Perfect, Mom, HomeGoods," I said, "throw it in our faces, why don't you."

Her answer was a snore. I turned to her. "Really, Mom?" The yellow light from the stores gave her cheek a sick color. Her jaw hung on her shoulder, her lips were parted. Grandpa's lips were open like that when he gave his last breath. I shut off the engine and pushed my hands in my pockets. The heat went away quickly. The only light was the yellow of the store windows and the parking lot lights.

"You really screwed up things this time, Mom. You *keep* doing it, and now..."

I didn't finish whatever I was thinking of saying. I opened the door, got out, locked the car, then reopened it and pulled a winter coat from our junk in the back and draped it over her. I locked it again, pocketed the keys, and headed for the store.

In the lobby between the inner and outer doors were three vending machines. I had a dollar. I flattened it, watched it disappear into the slot. Peanut butter and orange crackers, right? I wouldn't get full on them, but with six in the package, they'd take the longest to eat and were probably the most filling food on the menu, if they actually were food and not just chemicals. I wandered the aisles, eating one cracker after the other, slowly, to let them do their work. I took my time, trying not to be noticed. I touched stuff here and there. Cushions, sheets, coats, towels, soft things.

Then I passed a full-length mirror.

A ghost stared back. A sloppy ghost with shirttails dangling below his coat and orange crumbs on his chin. I should have gone as this on Halloween. What the heck! Ashy cheeks, dark eyes with gray around them, a face far off and hazy, a face in the distance. The idea that I'd ever wanted to touch this to Hannah's face!

The public address crackled and someone came on the microphone. I felt a jolt—had I taken anything? I looked at my hands. Nothing. They were empty.

A cheery voice said, "It is now seven forty-five. In fifteen minutes the store will close. Please bring your purchase up to the registers and have a good evening!"

How did it get so late? How long had I been wandering the aisles?

Someone laughed. A cashier. Sure, they were all going home. I suddenly thought of Mom in the cold car and hurried to the doors. The black night punched me when I pushed through them. I unlocked my door and slid inside. It was cold, but she had burrowed into the coat I'd left on her. I whispered to her. Nothing. I gave her a touch, then a shake; she snored louder. Are you kidding me? She was out cold, snoring like a tractor trying to start. She wasn't going to do this, was she? Go into a deep sleep right here? Make *me* sleep here? Cars were starting up around us, backing out, lining up, leaving the lot, driving away. "Mom, Mom, please?" Nothing. I started the car, the heater went on, blowing cold. The gas gauge was so near empty, I had to turn it off. I crawled into the back, kicked our junk to the floor, and huddled in a ball. Stupidly, I thought of Hannah again. What a jerk I am. An idiot. Gross and weird and stupid. I slapped my face. I can't tell you why. You know why.

To get her out of my mind I thought about those weird twins staring from the window. I thought about Josh's apple. I thought about the bum's apple. Then I thought about nothing.

Sleep was a long black cold runway that didn't end, until it suddenly snapped in half by a loud flicking and tapping on the steamed-up window nearest my head.

"Mom?" My neck wouldn't move. "Mom?" More stupid tapping at another window now. I arched up on my elbows. The windshield was pink. The front seat was empty. Mom was gone. What the—

"Who's in there?" said a voice. "Are you okay in there?"

With my frozen fingers, I cranked the back window down a crack. Ice crystals flaked off. The sky was light blue, turning pink. I blinked at a face surrounded by fur.

"What in the world? Did you...This car's ice cold. Did you *sleep* in there?"

My throat was dry as bone, my stomach hollow and gnawing at me, my head ringing, I couldn't speak. I'd spent the night in our car. Mom had left me in there. She let me go. She was dead. Maybe I was dead, too.

"Is there anyone I can call for you?" the furry man said. "The police? Is this even your car? Maybe I should call the police—"

"*What? No, no, no!*"

A distant voice, heels clicking fast. My brain was slow to pick up the clues, but I looked out beyond the furry man's shoulder to see someone coming toward the car.

"That's my son in there. He's all right. I was gone two seconds, for crying out loud!" It was Mom, all blustery, hurrying back, like she did at the diner in New Hampshire, like she does, all ready with a story. "We had a bit of car trouble, but we're fine—"

"He'll freeze out here!"

"Which is why I brought coffee, thank you. Cocoa, too. We'll try the new battery, warm up, and be on our way, thank you!"

I sat up, pushed cold fingers through frozen hair. She clicked the door locks and opened the passenger door. "Here, Josh, hot cocoa." She held out a cup to me.

I must have mentioned Josh when I talked about school. I took it up a notch. "Thanks, Sandra. I mean, Mom. I know you don't like me to call you by your first name."

Clumsy, for sure, but it worked on Fur Man.

"Josh. Sandra. You're both all right, then?" he said.

"Yes," I said, smiling at him. "We'll be going soon."

The man backed away, nodding. "Okay. All right. It's cold, is all."

"Thank you," Mom said, slipping into the driver's seat. "Thank you so much!"

She settled her coffee into the cup holder and started the car. It took a couple of tries before it turned over, but it did and we drove slowly away.

CHAPTER 32
WHAT NOW? WHAT MORE?

There was no question of my going to school that day. I guess neither of us could see the point.

Of all places, Mom drove us to the beach, stupid on a frigid day. We didn't talk for hours. What would we say? We had just spent a freezing night in our car. What was left? Huddling in doorways? Gutters?

I looked out the windshield. Cold, bleak endless water, rolling and rolling under heavy clouds. It's amazing how slowly the time can pass when you want it to be gone, and how it flies away when you try to hold it down.

That moment with Hannah at the library was so utterly in the past, I wondered if those ten minutes had ever happened. Maybe I had imagined the whole thing.

This—*this*—was what we were, Mom and me, in a cold car, in a barren lot where neither of us should be, overlooking the stone-gray water, smelling of ourselves, watching the day die in front of us, and too tired to feel anything but empty.

It was so dark in my eyes I thought it couldn't get worse.

Then Mom spoke, repeating words she'd used in the attic.

"It's time."

As cold as I thought I was, my blood froze solid. I turned to her.

"Mom, what now? What more...?"

She had hinted a couple of weeks ago that if she ran out of every other place, every other stinking place in the world, we might have to spend a night or two in a shelter before we bounced back to something real. Bouncing wasn't anything I understood anymore, and I knew we couldn't do it. A shelter sounded like death. Worse than death. A place of failure. A place for people who admitted they had hit the bottom.

She said it again now.

"I called two-one-one. This morning. You were sleeping. They have a room for us. It'll be warm. It'll be ready tonight. Someone's leaving. It's not far from here."

She stuttered all this out like she could no longer put a whole sentence together, like it was too cold to bother. I got it. I understood how and why she talked like that. You don't have enough strength or faith or whatever to say a whole sentence anymore. What was the point of making sense? What was the point of anything? There wasn't any. There was only us, like this. This was who we are.

"Honey, I'm...sorry..." She choked and practically fell into me, her arms around me, her cheeks wet and somehow warm.

"Okay, Mom. It's okay. We'll do it."

"Just for a day. Or two days. A week, tops. I'll get the job, I'm sure of it. My salary will kick in. In the meantime"—she sniffed—"your father will send us money."

Hearing that made me mad. "What does *he* have to do with anything?"

"He's trying to put some money together. He's really trying. I talked to him, and he agreed. It will take a few days, but he knows he has to do that—"

"He's always known it. What's different now?"

"—then we'll have a place again. I promise. My checks will start coming, we'll be fine. Get back on our feet. By Christmas we'll be in a brand-new place. I promise."

"Don't promise!"

But she kept talking so I tuned her voice out like I'd done so many times before.

Back when we were selling furniture to shops in Bridgeport, she'd driven us past one of the shelters. She'd slowed the car and wrinkled up her face as if we were

passing a prison. I remembered the people standing outside. Men mostly. A priest lady in a collar moving her
arms. Clouds of cigarette smoke. Shifting feet. The dark
tunnels where their eyes should be.

Now that was us. That was us, too.

CHAPTER 33
WHAT THEY CALL IT

"Welcome to the Hope Mission. I'm so glad you called."

The woman smiling in the office of the brick building said that when we entered the lobby. *Hope?* Seriously? Was *hope* anything at all but the flip side of hopelessness? Haven't we already decided that hope is just the flip side of hopelessness? And *Mission?* They call the shelter a mission, but it isn't a mission for people from just one religion. It's open to losers from all religions, a bad joke I kept to myself.

"I'm glad you called, Mrs. Hicks, and I'm happy to have a room open in one of our buildings. It's nearby. Welcome, Jeff."

"Hi."

She motioned to a pair of chairs and we sat across her cluttered desk. She saw me eyeing the piles of paper. "Paperwork. Emergency shelters are especially full when the weather turns cold."

There it was again. The cold.

"We actually live on the other side of town," Mom said, and I wondered what she thought that meant. "I'm getting a job very soon and this is just a little bump."

The woman nodded, but her expression told me she'd heard that before. "Perfect. Good. Most of our residents do stay for longer than a month."

"A month?" My chest buzzed.

"Sometimes. Our goal, of course, is to find permanent housing for everyone."

"Really, it's just a stop," Mom said, with a look at me.

"But not the last stop," the woman said, as if she'd heard that before, too. "Maybe it's silly, it's in our brochures, but we like to think of ourselves as a kind of greenhouse. I wrote it, so it *could* be silly. But it helps to know what we're about. Not just offering a room, but a place for people to grow into what they're capable of. Like seeds, in a way, if that's not too...but I can see by your faces that I may need to rewrite that?"

She paused to look at me. "The point is, right from the get-go you'll have help, a social worker assigned to you—"

"Do we need that?" Mom said, interrupting her. "It really won't be that long."

The lady nodded slowly. "I understand, but unstable living arrangements tend, I'm sorry to say, to keep going on, without help, and a social worker is the first step."

Emergency shelter. Greenhouse. Unstable living arrangements.

"We won't be here long," I said. Mom touched my hand.

The woman put her palms flat on the desktop. "Great. We love that. So. There are some questions, a few, just to help you move in. Jeff, I'd prefer you to stay for this, but if you don't want to, you can wait in the waiting room."

I looked at Mom. Her lips were tight.

"I'll stay."

"Perfect." From the top drawer of her desk, she took a form several pages long. She asked my age and what grade I was in and where I go to school. I told her.

"Maybe you don't know this," she said, "but it's mandated by the state that the school pick you up from here and bring you to school."

"A bus?" I said. "All the way down here?"

"Not a bus, a taxi. Or a car. But they'll come in the morning and drop you back."

"That..." I turned to Mom. "I don't want to do that. People will know, won't they? I don't want that. Mom, can you still drive me?"

She breathed out. "Yes. Sure. That's fine."

Next she asked about Mom's job and money situation, skills she might have, where we'd been staying since we left the house, how long in each place, and if there was a father in the picture. She asked about substance issues, which Mom tried to sidestep, but the lady wouldn't let her, and Mom pledged not to drink at the shelter. The lady said they would have to check our bags. Both of ours.

It hurt. It all hurt, the questions the lady had to ask and the answers Mom had to give. I realized only when it was over that we'd been holding hands.

"Great. Good." The lady smiled and dangled her car keys. "Follow me in your car, and we'll get you settled."

We followed her five short streets to a medium-sized L-shaped brick building and parked.

"You'll buzz yourselves in and out," she said as she keyed in a code and the door clicked open. "This used to be the old police station, as you'll see."

What? I wondered. Jail cells? No. But there was a heavy young man with a beard sitting behind a counter right inside the door, like they have in old cop shows.

"This was the sergeant's office," the lady said. The guy shook hands with us, welcomed me by name before the lady told him. They were expecting us.

"We're lucky you called when you did," she said as she took us through the halls. "We only have three rooms for families—mothers and children only—and they go quickly. Too quickly. Single men are upstairs. You'll never see them. Single women in the other wing." She stopped in front of a black door, unlocked it, and flicked on the light. Two twin beds, floor lamps, a dresser, and a changing table. Then she gave us two keys and offered us a box of toiletries, a loaf of bread, and jars of peanut butter and jelly.

"Thank you," I said. "This is great."

"Katie, our social worker, will call soon to arrange an appointment with you. For now, we'll let you get settled."

"Thank you," Mom said.

The lady meant to be kind and *was* kind and didn't talk down to us or to me. She nodded once, smiled at me, and left.

"Speaking of changing tables," I said, "where's Dad's check, anyway?"

"In the mail. He says. It smells like disinfectant in here. I guess it's all right."

"Hey, this is a greenhouse, remember?" I said. "Maybe we'll grow into trees by morning, with tree houses in them and we can live in those"—which meant who knows what, and I didn't want to mock the nice lady, but then Mom reminded me that Grandpa had had plans to build me a tree house but lost his leg instead. That cheered me right up.

That night was horrible.

The ceiling was gashed with slivers of streetlight, like the ceiling in the pink cottage so many nights ago. There were five slashes of light, not a lot, but I counted them over and over until I must have fallen asleep. It was warm, though, and I liked that we could lock our door at night. The bouncer at the sergeant's window meant no one would come pounding on our door or tapping our windows, so I was safe.

I was safe but ashamed that Mom had brought us here.

———

Maybe I did grow overnight, because by morning the room seemed airless and smaller than a closet. Plus I had peed in my sleep. I hadn't done that since Grandpa died. It wasn't much, but it was enough to soak my underpants, and because we had left most of our things buried in the car, I had only the one pair with me. It was either go commando or I don't know what, until this kid outside the bathroom saw me and said he uses the iron in the room off the little kitchen.

"To dry it before people come down for breakfast," he said. "I'm Jano. I do it for my brother when he pees and we didn't do laundry. Tad is five."

"Thanks," I said. "This isn't pee, it's..."

But I couldn't come up with anything before Jano added, "I pee myself sometimes."

I didn't know what to say then either, except: "Cool."

Which cracked him up.

Then he told me to rinse the stain out with soap and water before drying the underpants with the iron.

"Have you ever smelled plain hot dried pee?" he asked.

"Uh, no."

"You really don't want to."

Jano and Tad were really Janos and Tadeusz. After I dried my underpants, I had breakfast with them in the kitchen, where they told me their mother worked for the shelter while the three of them stayed there.

"She moves furniture and does carpentry. She's big," Tad said, puffing himself up and making a face. "She's saving to buy a car so we can drive to Ohio where our grandparents live."

"And where a job is waiting," Jano said softly. "Maybe. We hope."

Jano was cool. They'd been there three months. His father was somewhere he didn't know. I didn't want to lie to him so I didn't.

"My mom has problems with drinking and losing jobs and money and we lost our house. Which I've never said out loud before, but, you know, why lie about it?"

"Mommy used to do crack, but she's clean now," Tad said as if he'd learned the words listening to grown-ups. Then he added, "I like to be clean, but I don't like baths."

Talking to them, and especially Jano, was so regular. Jano got it. His story was different from mine but the same, too. He was nine. Tad laughed a lot at things Jano said and did. He nearly choked when I Groucho-walked around the table. Then he decided to do it, then it was all three of us.

When Mom came down to the kitchen, she was with a young woman with red hair and a clipboard. "I'm Katie. Hi, Jeff. Hi, kids!" Jano and Tad gave her little waves.

"Talk later, yes?" she said, looking at me and Mom.

Mom nodded, and Katie left.

"She seems nice," I said.

"Social worker," Mom whispered, then she started her fluttery thing, not wanting anyone to talk while she butterflied around. It got cold in there pretty quick.

———

I made it to school late because of traffic. Mrs. Ward, one of the counselors, was waiting by the doors. I suddenly got hot, my skin boiling, and my sweats started.

She smiled at me and tried to be casual. I smiled back.

"You've been late quite a few times, Jeff. Is everything all right?"

I started lying right away. "Yeah, yeah. Just we're remodeling at home and things are everywhere and my mom has car troubles some days. It's being fixed this afternoon. The car."

"Would you mind if I called her?"

More smiling. "Really. We're good. No more late days. I promise."

"I'll call her anyway, if that's all right with you."

There wasn't any way out of it. "Sure. After supper. When she's home from work."

As I walked away, it seemed like they'd suddenly

turned the ceiling lights up to a thousand. My skin got so hot, my face and chest burned. I had to squint, the hallways seemed so bright. My stomach was empty and raw and gnawing at me. I'd had eggs that morning at the shelter, but I guess they didn't last. The school knows. They know! But there was nothing I could do now. I tried to forget it and pretend life was normal.

When I drifted into Mr. Maroni's class, he was moving between the seats and you could tell he was happy to leave behind *Of Mice and Men*—a real bummer of a story, which I won't give away—and get to our new book, "A strange little novel set in Australia called *Pobby and Dingan*," that absolutely no one had ever heard of.

"Enchanting, unusual, and utterly alive masterpiece of only"—he checked the end of the book—"ninety-four pages! It is"—he added in an accent—"one of my *five-rit booooks evah!*"

It was supposedly about a girl's imaginary friends who go missing. I wanted to be them. I was so far behind in everything, I could barely follow what he was saying, but I did understand that something different was going on in the class now.

Ever since the Hannah *Mungo* thing, Mr. Maroni had changed. He was definitely excited about each new book, but he was also quieter, more patient with us. It was like we all understood that because one of *us*, not him, had discovered something, it was both important and strangely sad. It didn't matter that Hannah had said she was happy that *This isn't everything* and *I'm not stuck here*, it sort of crushed you and made you feel hopeless somehow. Like being happy was only wishful thinking. I don't know what it was exactly, but now the class made me sad and I think it made everyone sad.

Now and then it seemed like Mr. M wanted to talk to me—did he know, too?—but I ducked out before he could. Ducking out on teachers, hard to do, but I did it.

Later I saw Hannah out of class. Well, she saw me. It was one of the days I didn't eat. I was passing quickly through the cafeteria to get to the courtyard where I hung out on the bench behind the tree.

"Jeff!" she said.

I looked over. She smiled like she did at the public library that time. I went over, wondering how I smelled. I didn't sit down. She was eating off a tray in front of her. Another tray was at the empty seat next to her.

"Sit," she said. "Carly went home and left me her lunch. I'd already bought mine. I don't know what to do with it. Sit?"

I looked at the tray. Food untouched. "Who's Carly?"

"Carly. Short. Cornrows?" She wiggled her fingers over her ears.

I looked around. "Her whole lunch?"

"If you don't want it, I hear they give the uneaten food to the sixth graders."

"You funny," I said, and pulled the tray across the table to me and sat.

She smiled. "So what do you think of our little friends Pobby and Dingan?"

I tried not to eat the grilled cheese too fast. "I'm siding with the brother that they aren't real. Maybe. But the book is named after them, so I don't know."

She chuckled. "It's another *voice* book."

"He loves them," I said.

She cracked through a stalk of celery. "I think I like it. It's strange, but." Which was Australian talk, to put words at the end of the sentence that belonged at the beginning. "I think it gets sad, though, so don't tell me if you read ahead."

"I... won't...."

The sealed cup of pudding, the unopened chocolate milk, the cut carrots and celery.

"I don't want to read it fast. Not that anybody can. Trying to figure out the lingo."

I didn't get it. There were choices in the cafeteria line. The food on my tray was exactly the same as the food on her tray. My face suddenly got hot and then my whole body did and I caught a whiff of myself. I pushed the chair out and looked around.

"What's wrong?"

"I know..." I stood up. "I know I'm not the sharpest tool, but did you... did you buy me lunch?"

Her eyes, wide and brown and looking straight into my face. "What?"

"Don't give me that. This isn't *Carly's* lunch.... There is no *Carly*.... This is..." I stepped back into someone's chair.

"Carly Emory," she said. "She got sick...."

I went away fast. Somewhere. I forget where. My body took me and I wasn't in control. Black knives spun in my eyes. Twice I turned the other way when I saw her in the hall. I think it was twice. I took the long way through the building. The day ended that way. The counselor didn't call, or maybe she tried the old home number. I was glad the weekend came. Mom couldn't wait to leave the shelter for the day each day, telling me she needed to do this and that. She dodged the social worker when she could. I stayed, spent time with Jano and Tad, told them about Pobby and Dingan. Mostly I holed up in the room and wondered how invisible friends can disappear.

On Monday, I was still burning inside and hid in the bathroom when I spotted Mrs. Ward in the hall. A teacher found me; I pretended to be sick. Like pretend Carly.

I skipped Tuesday. The next day I saw Hannah in the hall again, as if she lived there, hunting me. It was late afternoon. She was coming toward me, but even though my underwear was clean I could still smell pee on me and couldn't talk to her and felt I was going to throw up, so I ducked into another lavatory. She had shamed me. I hated her for what she had done. She knew about me.

My face in the mirror shocked me. Way worse than the night I slept in our car. Sunken cheeks. Weird white lips. Greasy hair. Why hadn't Mom told me I looked like this? My ears were hot and red, my skin too tight for my skull. I was staring in the mirror at my face and neither of us was me. I hung on to the edge of the sink with both hands, bony and bloodless as my face, trying to breathe. From now on, I wouldn't do anything other than move from here to there. I didn't need the attention. I needed the opposite of attention now. I lived in a shelter.

The bell rang, and I was outside before it stopped. Hannah was still in the hall. I pushed by her—"Jeff. Jeff!"—and kept my eyes down. I wanted to disappear.

To be not anywhere.

But Mom was waiting in the lot, crying with good news.

CHAPTER 34
ROLLER COASTER

"I got the job!" She hugged me from behind the wheel even before I was all the way in. "I told you! I told you!"

I tried to harden myself into stone.

"Did you hear me? I got the job."

"You...got the job?"

"I got the job!" She laughed through her tears as she pulled jerkily around the circle and away. "Their first choice was wrong. She looked good on paper, but I didn't like her. She was snotty when I asked her where she'd worked. They found out and good riddance!" She whooped. "I start on Monday. I won't get my first paycheck for two weeks, but I think we'll have just enough until then."

"Enough for what? A bigger room at the shelter?"

"We're never going back there, Jeff. Spend Thanksgiving in a shelter? No way. A hotel. A better one. A really nice one! We can swing it, Jeff. Your father finally sent a check. More money this time."

"He did? How much?"

"Enough, Jeffie. I'm going to keep this job, I know I am."

She was always doing this, putting on a face to make me feel better. I didn't have the strength anymore to call her out on it, so I went along, pretending to be the old Jeff.

"Will the hotel have a heated pool this time?"

"Two pools!" she said. "And both of them will be in our room! I'll make sure of it!"

We drove to the mission, where we collected our stuff and signed out way more quickly than we checked in. The nice lady stood in the little sergeant's room, smiling at us, at me, happy that things were looking up for us. I could tell she wanted to say more, and would have if it was just me, but my mother was all jerky movements, trying to distract everyone.

The lady did manage to say, "Good for you both. And you, Jeff. Good luck."

"Thank you," I said, ashamed I hadn't bothered to learn her name.

I searched for Jano and found him and Tad in the little library, reading to each other, only Tad was just pretending and making up words. When I told them I was going, leaving the shelter, Tad's little face broke apart.

I'd pretty much only seen him laugh since we got there, but now he had noticed his big brother's shoulders drop, and I guess he knew what that meant. Jano brought himself back enough to make a half smile and tickle his brother's armpits.

"Good," Jano said to me. "Cool. See you around."

"Probably not," my mother said from the doorway.

Which was so rude, I knew that somewhere, some-time, she must have had a drink, or was itching to get one, and I wondered what world she thought she was liv-ing in and why she wanted me to be there, too. I shook Jano's hand, then I shook Tad's little hand.

"Happy Thanksgiving, guys," I said.

"You too," said Jano, and Tad's chin started to quiver again.

Driving away, Mom kept on saying that we weren't like them, we weren't their kind, that it was obvious we were different from all the people there, until I told her to stop.

"We *are* like them," I said. "And they're like every-body else. Good people who don't have good luck. I liked that lady. She was so kind. She was nice, always nice."

"Uh-huh," she said. "Well, our luck is changing, except it's not luck, is it? I got the job. That's skill." Which meant I have no idea what.

When we got to the second hotel, it actually *was* bet-ter than the first. It cost more and the room was bigger. I felt a little scared when I saw the gleaming bathroom. Really, this is our room? After the shelter, we get to live here? Spend Thanksgiving in a real suite. Two rooms, two firm beds. Music playing from a speaker. An enormous flat-screen TV. Is this right? Is this even real?

Mom thought we'd just left a prison, but maybe she was wrong, because dinner that night felt like a prisoner's last meal.

You eat great, but only once.

Mom and me, we were lucky. We ate great for five whole days.

CHAPTER 35
MOMMY, OH, MOMMY

It was the afternoon of our sixth day at the new hotel. Mom couldn't pick me up after school, so I took the bus to my old stop, hopped a city bus down Madison Avenue, then walked the rest of the way to the hotel. It had been dark and cold all day. It was nearly suppertime and just starting to rain when I walked into the lot.

Before I got to the room, I saw someone hunched in a ball against the ground floor wall like some kind of dead spider. Hearing my footsteps, she moved suddenly.

"Mom?"

She looked up. "Jeff!"

"Mom, what are you doing out here—"

"The social worker's been here!" she said. "Sniffing around. I slipped her...slipped away from her and her stupid clipboard!"

"Who? Katie?"

Mom smelled as if she'd fallen into a vat of wine. She sounded like it, too. "Why is she following us? Getting all nosy?"

"She's probably checking on how we're doing. You're wet. Let's go inside."

"How we're doing? How I'm screwing up is what she's after. How does she even know where we are?"

"Mom, come on. Let's go in."

"We're in Bridgeport here stealing against the town and they fire and jail people our town knows stealing..." She snagged my hand with hers; her fingers were wet. I couldn't figure out where her sentences started and where they were going.

"What do you mean, Mom?" I helped her to her feet. "Who stole what—"

"Us! This!" She slapped my backpack. "School!"

"What about school? You're not making any sense."

She stood up straight, or tried to, then glanced behind her as if she expected someone. "Because you didn't want the free ride to school. It's like lying. Oh, and your counselor called me today. You should have heard the line I gave her!" As if that meant anything.

"It's late, Mom. Let's get to the room—"

"Shut up and listen. If that social worker found me... like this...you'll go straight into DCF!"

"What's DCF?"

"Department of Children's Families. Foster care—ever heard of that?"

"They wouldn't do that. Why would they? We would have heard about it." I moved her slowly to the stairway. The elevator was too far away. "Up here..."

"You don't know that! So you need to keep your mouth shut about me. I heard you talking to that kid. He's mad you left. He'll tell. They tell to get ahead."

"That's...Mom, that's crazy. Jano won't tell anybody."

"His pip-squeak of a brother, then."

"Mom, stop."

What came to me as I was saying this was what my dad had said. I was thirteen and I shouldn't be talking this way. Like an adult trying to dodge the law or whatever. Then, on the heels of that thought came another. That's what I had become, isn't it? I was the man of my two-person family. I wasn't a kid anymore.

"It's that bum. Andrade. He told the social worker."

"Whoa, Mom, you're talking nutty."

"I told them about him! All those questions! The bum! Help me up, help me."

"He's not a bum, Mom," I said. And he wasn't. He was a guy who rented houses and wanted people to pay their rent. We're the bums. Kid, man, bum.

"Okay, Mom. Just...let's get to the room."

She left it at that for a few steps, then said, "I'm not

212

having you change schools every other semester. I had to do that when I was a kid when Daddy moved, and I hated it. I don't want you to hate school like I did."

Too late, I wanted to say. I kept my mouth shut.

Then the dumbest thing happened. We were one step from reaching the landing when she dug into her pocket. She pulled out one of those personal wine bottles they sell to make it easy to sneak a drink.

"Mom, what the heck—"

"I'm done with this, Jeffie. Done! Let them see that!" And she lobbed it at a trash bin a few yards away. The bottle made it perfectly into the bin, with no sound all.

The bottle made it, Mom didn't.

Her foot was halfway between steps when she slipped. I tried to grab her arm, but her left leg buckled under her right one, her shoe slid off, and she fell two steps, then there was a snap. She screamed an ugly scream that didn't bring anyone running because she screamed it into my shoulder. She hung with all her weight on me, crying that something had broken, her ankle or her foot.

I lifted her, my hands under her armpits. She wasn't big, but she was a deadweight. We dragged ourselves up to the landing, nearly falling twice, and over to our door.

Tugging my keycard from my rear pocket, I swiped it into the lock. A light greened, the door clicked, we pushed into the room. I slid her off me onto the bed.

"I should...I should never have let you see me take

a drink," she groaned into the pillow. "Years ago. Never should have."

"Lift your head." She didn't, so I squeezed a pillow halfway under it.

"I never used to. When you were small I'd wait until you were in bed. Then I did it once, and you didn't notice and I kept doing it more and more."

"I noticed. And you can stop drinking anytime, you know."

"So why haven't I? What if I can't—"

"I'm getting some ice."

I left the room with the plastic bucket they put in the rooms to help you drink, and stumbled down the hall to the noisy ice maker, my blood freezing in my veins. The sound of cubes falling into the bucket was like bricks dropping on my head. When I got back, she was breathing funny. Big rapid gulps.

"Mom, are you choking?" Her ankle was already puffy and blue. Her eyes closed suddenly, and she breathed out a long, rattling breath.

"Holy crap! I'm calling an ambulance. Mom. Mom!" I patted her cheek, softly at first, then harder until she opened her eyes and started sobbing.

"Don't call—"

"I'm calling. Where is your phone?" I clawed into her bag, grabbed her phone, and typed in 911.

"No! They'll take you away! I'm drunk."

"I don't care!"

But when the call connected and they demanded who I was, I gave them only basic information. I was afraid to tell them much more. "A lady broke her ankle and needs an ambulance. I...no, I don't know her name. She's in... room 2031..." And the rest. "Just hurry!" I said, and hung up.

"You shouldn't have done that."

"And watch you die on the bed?"

"Jeffie!" she said. "Here. Here!" She shoved her change purse at my hands, then slipped back to the headboard, banging her head.

"You need to get out of here. They'll take you away from me! Get out of here!"

There was a distant siren. I stuffed more pillows behind her head, under her foot. I thought of my grandfather. A car door slammed. She swung a limp hand at me.

"Mom, please—"

But I got it. I thought I did. The medics would bring her to the hospital. They'd read her blood alcohol level. *Unfit mother.* I'd be in the foster system before I woke up. But what was I supposed to do now, right now? Hide from the police? You can't do that.

"Go!" she pleaded. "Leave the phone they track those things get out. Get out!"

I covered her with blankets, snatched two bottles of booze off the dresser, and went.

I hurried down the corridor and onto the landing, surprised to find my backpack still on my back. It wasn't even six, but black and cold. No moon. No stars.

I dumped the bottles in a trash container and ran off into the shadows.

CHAPTER 36
RUNNING ON EMPTY

I stopped running when an ambulance swung in through the puddles, whooping one last time. From the far side of the lot I saw its doors fly open and a woman jump to the ground. She and a guy hurried up the stairs while the driver unloaded a gurney. Guests came out of their rooms to see.

A heavy black SUV rolled in, its lights flashing. Cops. I knew they were there to help my mom. Cops do other stuff besides arrest people, but they scared me. Mom scared me. How long could they not know that I was missing?

It was insane to run away.

A few slow minutes ticked by before they brought her down slantwise on the gurney, not caring about me, only her. The sirens started up a minute or two after that. I guessed they'd bring her to Bridgeport Hospital, which was the closest. My blood rushed in my ears. I started walking backward until the shadows swallowed me completely. Everything was dreamy, blurred, muffled. Where to go, where to hide. A place to be, a quiet place, to sort it out.

I made my way to the corner, then headed left for three blocks to where I knew there was an uptown bus stop. It was raining heavily now. I tugged my hoodie tight.

There was a lady there. A man and a little girl. They said things.

"Where's your mother and father?" the woman said, not nosy, just matter-of-fact.

"I'm...I'm meeting my mother," I said.

She stepped away, her eyes still fixed on my face. "Good luck, son."

A roar and a squeal. The bus doors shushed open. I climbed up after the lady, scraped Mom's change purse for enough coins, and took a seat. The bus drove into traffic slowly, like it was dragging a block of concrete.

Rain clawed the windows. My ghost reflection. Shiny streets. Everything buzzed like chain saws in my ears. The route wasn't direct, but near enough. Nobody asked me what was up. I guess I had that kind of face. Skin pulled tight on the bone. Maybe I looked older than thirteen. No one wanted to know.

I jumped out five blocks from Belmont, traced the streets up to my house, my old house. They wouldn't be working at night, would they? It was probably empty.

So what?

So it was my house.

But was it? The sad gray house, the house I don't belong to?

Whatever. I was a ghost, moving like a ghost on the sidewalk, invisible among the raindrops. The FOR RENT sign was gone. Had someone moved in? From where I stood on the sidewalk, you could see through to the lights in the backyard beyond ours. Good. The rooms were still empty. I was alone.

Up the dark path to the front door, up the steps. The wind rose, it rained harder. I knew where the puddles would be and avoided them. The toes of my sneakers and my socks were already wet enough. I heard noises from the end of the street. People talking. Teenagers. I didn't move. The voices stopped. A car pulled away. I was out of the glare of the streetlight. It looked like no one was standing on the step where I was standing.

I didn't bother to try the knob. The welcome mat was gone. A smell came from the gap around the door. Leaning, I peeked in the front window to make sure. The living room was dead. I pulled my hood forward; it was soaked from the cold steady drops.

Down the steps and past the garage to the back door. Locked. I looked up at my old room. I couldn't breathe. The window was cracked open. So were others. Why? The smell. They had painted inside and were airing the smell out of it.

I hoisted myself onto the railing. It was slippery. Grabbing the edge of the low roof over the door, I elbowed up, then crawled on my stomach to my window. The sash was up several inches. Rain beaded the inside sill.

The screen was tight but I jiggled it until the tab was visible. Fishing into my pack, I pulled out a card. Mom's debit card. It was good for something at least. I flicked the tab, slicing my finger, but the screen came loose. I laid it on the shingles and grabbed the sill with both hands to pull myself into my old room. I reattached the screen behind me and pushed the window down. I was inside.

The floor was waiting to be sanded, but the walls had just been painted. Drop cloths and cans and brushes and roller pans were scattered here and there, and the ceiling light was down and lying on its side in a cardboard box, its wires like ghost fingers coiling down from the attic. I mopped up the rain with one of the loose rags, wiped a smear of finger blood from the sill, and sat in the middle of the floor, crossing my legs. I hunched under my hoodie, wet and cold.

My room.

I closed my eyes and imagined it before everything was taken away. My desk. The old chair. The dresser. My bed. Oh, my bed. Why did I even come here? To be back in my old life? Except this wasn't my room anymore. It wasn't anything. The soul of me was gone from it. It was a grave. A hotel room was better. The storage locker. The car. The air was thick with paint fumes and didn't smell of living people.

I suddenly thought of the furnace in the basement. It had to be fixed by now. Even if it wasn't, there was the clothes dryer. I yanked off my hoodie, shirt, and pants on the way downstairs, found that those floors had been done, adding to the smell. I tossed my clothes in the dryer, setting it to maximum heat. I sat on top, my butt and legs warming, until I wondered if the workmen were keeping anything in the fridge.

Some haul—a squirt bottle of hot sauce, two cans of beer, an unopened bag of sauerkraut, and a bowl of shriveled cherry tomatoes. I couldn't see any connection. I ate the tomatoes. My empty stomach squirmed. Too much acid. My previous meal was cereal and two containers of cream. Mom liked her morning coffee white-white.

The dryer buzzed. My clothes were dry and hot. They felt so good. I went back upstairs to my room and felt like crying. Minutes passed of doing nothing but breathing in that little room before I realized my head was pounding. The chemicals from the floor and the paint were slamming my head, burning the backs of my eyes.

I made my way downstairs. The empty living room. Grandpa's room. *He was everything. So many things. Always moving.* His room was a tomb now. My throat choked me.

I sat in the doorway, remembering. *Daddy, oh,*

Daddy. I wondered what was happening with Mom right then and how scared she must be. Looking back, as much time as I'd spent with her, all I'd seen was the way she was acting, not the way she was inside. She was so scared and she loved me so much. And she hurt.

She tried, every day she tried, but she was sick, sick with drinking and by not being smart when she was that way, and by being scared. She loved me so much and hurt so much and made mistakes.

I balled up my hands in my pockets, knowing I was going to leave right then and make my way to the hospital to be with her, when there was a sharp knock at the back of the house.

I swung around. An arm moved outside the kitchen window next to the door. A face appeared, with hands cupped against the glass. I froze.

Rich? What's *he* doing here? Go away. *Go away!*

After a few seconds—it seemed so much longer—he tapped the window. I still didn't move. Finally, he called through the door.

"Jeff. Let me in. I'm getting soaked out here."

CHAPTER 37
WINNER OF EVERYTHING

Planting my foot inside it, I unlocked the back door and pulled it in partway.

"Rich, just go home—"

It wasn't Rich. It was Tom Bender. The face I'd seen every day since third grade, then not again until last week or the week before or whenever.

He was squinting dumbly at me as the rain pelted his head. I swore at him.

"What are you doing here?" I said.

"Me? What are *you* doing here? Let me in."

The great Tom Bender, boyfriend of Courtney, winner of everything. He was dripping, shivering. I slid my foot aside and he came in.

"Wipe your stupid feet." I kicked over a rag with my foot. "This is a new floor. How did you even know I was here?"

He got most of the puddle, walking the rag around

under both feet like a prisoner in ankle cuffs. "I was at Rich's house—"

"Was he poisoning you against me?"

He stopped. "What? No—"

"No, no, of course not. Because nobody does that, right? Well, you can just"—and I did that thing with my finger that the lady did in New Hampshire when she saw me on her private road. The *rotate* move.

"Are you stirring something? Is it soup? What kind?"

"You've seen the freak, now go back to your friends."

"Rich's mom was supposed to look out for me after school. My parents are away in different places."

"Why are you even talking to me?" I said. "I hate you!"

He paused, then went on like he hadn't heard me. "But his mother went out, and Rich's sister's boyfriend is over, and Rich is gross sick with a cold. It's like being alone. He told me you left your house. I wanted to see for myself. What's going on?"

I looked at him, giving me that same face he used to, half all open and friendly, half wondering about something, and I hated it, couldn't stand to see it, but a heavy weight collapsed on me. Seriously, my body rippled all the way to the floor with exhaustion. I couldn't muster a lie, not just then. It was different from not lying to Jano, because he knew I was living the same life he was. This was different, Tom was nobody to me, but I still couldn't lie. Lying was useless. I didn't want to fight. I was too tired. I had nothing left.

"My mother got...She lost her job. Two months ago, almost. Month and a half. But she didn't pay the rent long before that, so we had to leave...."

"Whoa. Where are you living?"

"Somewhere. Nowhere. Hotels. Mom's friend for a week. Since then, places, here and there. A shelter for a few nights. Our car. Just...places."

It was a sad list when I said it out loud, and he cursed under his breath the way he never used to. "Man, I'm sorry. This stinks. I'm sorry."

I looked around. The shiny floor was moving from the rain crying down the window.

"Does anybody know?" he asked. "At school?"

I thought of Hannah, made her face vanish. "No. I'm too good at keeping secrets."

"Where's your mother now? I mean, is she okay?"

"My mother? Okay? No. She's drunk. She's a drunk. She drank when I was at St. Catherine's, and it's worse now. It's why she lost all her jobs. Plus, she broke her foot. Or her ankle, I don't know. They took her to the hospital tonight." My eyes burned from the smell. "She told me to hide from the police. Stupid idea. Once they figure out she was drunk, they'll come for me anyway. I'll have to leave my lousy school, become a foster kid who knows where, with a mom in jail, so just...just go away...."

"No way. They'll figure something out."

"Yeah, what? What exactly?" I mocked him. "You don't know anything. She screwed up so royally, maybe I *should* hide."

"Good plan, but there must be a better place. How can you stand the smell here?"

"That's my business. Go away, will you?"

All I wanted to do was drop to the floor and sleep.

Instead of going away, he pretended not to hear again, turned, and squeaked open the basement door. It was the same old squeak as when he used to come over. He peered down the stairs. Ignoring everything, he went all the way to the bottom.

The light switch clicked, and I heard another sharp curse under his breath. I pulled my sleeve over my eyes, sniffed up, and went down, too. No old couch, no piles of comics on the floor, no TV. Another dead, empty room. Whatever I might remember about it had been vacuumed away.

"We hung out here so much after school," he said. "So many hours. It's crazy."

And it popped out of me. "I felt so good when I was down here."

He grinned. "With me? Right? You felt good because I was here?"

"What are you being all funny for? I hate you. Get out of here."

I was mad and flicked the light out on us, then trotted back upstairs—where I heard an engine idling and the sharp crackle of a police radio.

CHAPTER 38
LEAVING

I stopped mid-step and listened.

He bumped me from behind. "Hey, use all the stairs—"

"Shh!"

A light flared suddenly through the front window across the dining room and against our old kitchen cabinets. It moved along the counter and went out. The front doorknob twisted back and forth. There was a tap at the window.

"Who's that?" he whispered. "Is it the landlord?"

"Will you shut up!"

The beam of light passed across the kitchen wall again, then fell. Darkness. A few seconds later, the side doorknob was jostled. I pulled the basement door closed except for a crack. The light sliced in the side window now and passed through to the living room.

"Did you tell Rich you were coming?" I whispered. "Did his mother send the cops?"

"She's not there, remember?"

"Whatever. This is breaking and entering!"

"You broke in. I was invited."

"Invited? 'Oh, I'm all wet! Please help me, please!'"

"I didn't say—"

"Shh!"

The radio yakked again, farther away this time, and a car door thumped. Two car doors. Voices from the front of the house.

"They'll call the landlord," I said.

He nudged my arm. "Out the back."

I gave him a look. "What?"

"They're in front," he said. "Out the back—hurry!"

I crouched and dashed across the kitchen floor, carefully unbolted the back door, and push-pulled it inch by inch until it was free. Cold rainy air. No voices. Onto the steps, closing the door, then across the yard, slowly, so I wouldn't splash or slip on the wet grass. One yard, the next, and the next. He was still with me.

"Go back to Rich's," I said. "This is dumb. I'm going to the hospital to see my mother, and don't tell him anything."

"What are you afraid of—"

The thin beam of a powerful flashlight flicked through a

hedge behind him. A voice calling. Another siren whooped a couple of streets away.

"Go!" I said. I pushed him away and he fell on his butt in the soaked grass. I left him and ran through a bank of hedges to a short curving street and slid in a puddle, soaking both shoes completely. I hurried up the sidewalk as quickly as I could to the top of a small rise and down the other side. Cars approached quickly.

Someone hissed from the corner. It was him, coming around the opposite way.

"What is your problem?" I shouted. "Get out of here—"

"They almost got me!" he said. "What do I do now?"

"'Help me, help me!'" I said, mocking him again. "Look, just go. You didn't do anything wrong yet, so go!" I started off, but a bunch of sirens crisscrossed each other in front of and behind us. I swore. Then he swore. Then I swore again.

"Let's just go to the hospital," he said. "My dad'll pick us up from there."

"You're deadwood. Look at you—"

"Look at *me*? I got here faster than you did!"

"You're such a jerk," I said.

"You are."

His lame comeback, like he couldn't tell I hated him and hated the cold, the night, my house, my mother, me, everything. I swore again and started walking fast through backyards toward downtown, miles away. *We* started walking fast. The dummy wouldn't leave. Sirens whined, but farther away now. The temperature was dropping fast. It was stupid. The mess of my life was getting messier.

I stopped in somebody's soggy brown garden. "I need to get my bearings. Hold on."

A phone tinkled. He dug in his pocket and pulled out a pink case.

"It's my mother's phone," he said. "Hello? Dad? Finally. When do you think you'll be home?" He held it flat so I could hear. There was a lot of honking on the phone.

"It'll be a couple more hours because of the snow and this traffic." His father's voice, tinny and far away. "I'm going to try to drive through it before the storm reaches you. Can you put Rich's mom on the phone?"

He looked at me. "I'm...I'm with Jeff now...."

"Jeff?" his father said. "What? Why? Never mind, put *his* mother on."

"She's...out...for a while. We're good."

"Does Rich's mother know where you are? Tell her if you haven't. Okay, it's rolling again. Mommy's not starting until late tomorrow. Stay where you are. I'll pick you up at Jeff's. Gotta go."

"Be safe!" Tom said as his father hung up.

I shook my head. "You'll twist into knots to not lie, won't you?"

"It's a gift. I have others."

I wanted to laugh, but I couldn't. I didn't want to hear my voice. I didn't want to hear his voice either. He reminded me of so much it twisted my insides. I hurried off across the yard, then across another to a street a block away from the main one. He followed me, of course. The air was black now, with the rain coming fast and hard. I was soaked through. Every now and again I wrung out my hood, and icy rain slid down my back.

It was so much fun.

CHAPTER 39

IT WAS WHAT IT WAS

For the next hour, the rain spat like bullets. Rivers sliced along the gutters and overflowed the storm drains with mounds of rolling water. Nobody sane would walk in it. We walked in it. One minute poured into the next. We were out of backyards now, sloshing down side streets. I hated that he was with me, stuck to me. I wished it were Hannah, as bad as I'd left it with her. Or nobody. Nobody would be better.

"My feet are soaked," he said as we cut through one side street after another. "And frozen. Wet feet make you feel colder than dry feet at the same temperature. Did you know that?"

I said nothing.

"Really, wet cold is worse than dry cold," he said. "Neat, huh, how being on the street teaches you physics?"

"On the street? What is this, like your big adventure? Tagging along with a loser into the creepy parts of

Bridgeport at midnight? You're all the same, using me to pretend you're risky or whatever. Rich does it, Hannah, all of you."

"What? No." He walked a few steps behind me. "And it's actually not midnight. It's like eight something." He pulled out his phone. "Eight twenty-one. Who's Hannah?"

"Keep quiet."

He wouldn't. "There's something really hideous called trench foot, did you know that? From the trenches in World War One. It happened to soldiers who tramped around with wet feet in their boots all the time. Tramping in trenches."

"Dictionary," I said. "You're a dictionary."

"Wikipedia, Mrs. Tracy says."

"So you talk in class now?"

"And some of them had to have their feet cut off because the skin died and there was gangrene. From the water always in the bottoms of the trenches."

Gangrene. Black dead skin. I wondered if Grandpa was watching me, wondering what the heck I was doing in my life.

Slogging and slogging, I pushed on, hoping I'd see a dim glow in the distance that would be the hospital. I knew it sat on a hill, huge and blazing with sick people. Grandpa had gone there for his operations and for his failing heart. The air was gray, thick with rain. No hospital. There was no way to see that far.

I sank inside. "We're, like, hours away from the dumb place."

"My parents had a big thing last week," he said out of nowhere.

"What?"

"An argument. About money."

"Too much?"

He could have said a thousand things, called me an idiot or a jerk, but he didn't, just walked past me, then stopped to let me lead. It was quiet for a while. Then he said, "My dad only works three days a week. For two months now. He started by telling us it'll pick up again, but he doesn't say that anymore. They did that to him just before the holidays, you believe it?"

How stupid of me, not even wondering why his father had been doing yard work on a weekday. Two and two, numbskull. "I saw him, raking, in the middle of the day. I didn't get it. . . ." Then I started to add *Sorry*, but I couldn't make the sound, not to him.

He scanned around suddenly as if he'd just woken up. "Hey, where are we? Is this, like, the abandoned-warehouse district? Do you even know? I think we took the wrong street or something."

It took me a second. "No. One more block, I think, then right. We'll circle the parking lots to keep off the sidewalks so we don't get picked up for wandering the streets or whatever. Pay attention. If your dad loses his job altogether, you might end up doing this someday. Learn from the master."

"And you had a problem with me being funny. You should do stand-up on TV."

"I can't stand up on the TV," I said. "My mom sold it."

"You're killing me."

"I'm trying."

I realized by the stinging in my nose what I'd lost when Tom and I stopped hanging out together. He was the only one who had anything going on. I'd been a jerk about lots of things. So had he. Or maybe he hadn't. I don't even know. He was a pain in the eye sometimes, but maybe not as much of a jerk as I was. As I am. Stuck here.

"You and that girl," I said.

He turned his face to me, his eyes half-hidden under his soaked fleece hat. "Courtney? We're just friends."

"No. The other one. Jessica Feeney."

He burrowed into his jacket. "I don't want to talk about her. Not with you."

"Have you seen her since she left St. Catherine's?"

"I don't want to talk about it."

"Have you talked to her at least?" He didn't answer. "You have."

"Is that the way or not?" He pointed left at a street of flickering lampposts.

I looked in both directions, then over my shoulder.

A car was coming slowly down the street and I was suddenly afraid. We were too visible, a couple of kids alone. "Keep walking to the stoplight. Like we know exactly where we're going."

"You mean we don't?"

The car passed, rolled to the corner, then turned without stopping. Bad driver. Or just lost. Hard to tell. We went on. And on.

Then Tom scraped to a stop behind me. "Are you humming?"

I half turned. "It's a gift."

"No, listen. What's that noise?"

I lowered my hood and heard a high-pitched electrical whining. "A herd of dragons?"

"That was my guess, but why in Bridgeport?"

I shrugged. "The apocalypse starts here."

"Oh, right. My dad said it might."

How was it possible to talk this way? How could *I* talk this way? As if we were still best pals. As if he hadn't dumped me last year. Except I already knew that was wrong. I dumped him just as fast because he was friends with Jessica Feeney, and I thought he lied to me and liked being with her more than with me. I don't know. A lot happens. Parents lose jobs, they drink booze, things fall apart. Now I'm on the street with him at night in the cold rain and I'm still falling to the bottom, so whatever.

He stopped dead.

"Why do you keep stopping?" I said. "Stop stopping!"

"Jessica," he said, and didn't say anything else.

I looked at him. His face was dripping. "Look. Whatever. I don't need to know."

"She's not better," he said. "I saw her. I went to Boston with my mom. I mean she's the same, not better, not worse. She still has problems with her lungs. All the smoke and chemicals in the car when it burned." He paused. "You were so mean to her."

I took a breath, couldn't answer. Because of all the water on his cheeks, I didn't know if he was crying. I remembered her scarred face. I'd tried to forget it all these months, the whole past year, but her face had never left me and here it was again, the opposite of Hannah's face.

"Okay," I finally said. "Well...I hated when you lied to me."

"You were mean to her," he said, "but that's not even the thing. We were all mean. Me too."

"What?"

"The way we stared at her, thought things about her, were scared of her. It was just...we were so lame. Or worse, we treated her like she shouldn't be there."

"Well, you talked to her," I said. "You were her friend...."

"I didn't do anything. I barely said anything to her.

But she knew people didn't want to be with her. She expected it, to be alone all the time. Isn't that just so nuts?"

"Well, but you went to her house."

"Yeah," he said. "Big deal. I don't know, I don't know what I'm saying—"

I stared down the blurry street. "We should keep going."

He didn't move. "I was actually trying to say something before. Things sort of ended with you and me because, I don't know..."

"Because you lied to me? I get it. It doesn't matter—"

"We all lied!" he said. "And it was like I tricked myself into thinking you were the jerk. That was so easy, right? Being mad at you. Jessica told me this later, when I saw her. She said I did to you what you did to her."

"What?"

"The same thing."

"The same thing what?"

"You were mad at her because she was easy to be mad at, coming into our class all burned and ugly. Just like it was easy for me to be mad at you because I was so good to her and you weren't."

My chest had a weight on it. "I don't know what you mean. We should walk." And I tried to walk, but he kept talking and I kept listening.

"I only saw the junk you did, not the junk you had

to live with. So I thought it was okay to not do stuff with you. It was only okay for me. Not for you. I dropped you like stones off a cliff. I cut you out of my life."

"Whatever. I moved on. You moved on. It was what it was."

He jammed his eyes shut. "I can't stand it. You. On the streets. This . . . this is real . . . a horror story. I mean, it's not your fault, or anybody's, but it's so stinking lousy—"

"It's actually your fault," I said as a joke, but my throat choked me, and he started blubbering into his hands.

"C-come on," I said. "I screwed up. I was a jerk. I keep being one. You had your stuff. We were both . . . you know . . . just never mind. I don't get any of it. We're here now, so let's just go."

"No, you go. You go. I'll stay here."

"You'll stay here? Here?" I looked at the rain and the cars and the shadows and I shivered. "Without me you'll be dead by—what time is it?"

He checked his phone. "Nine thirteen."

"By quarter after nine you'll be dead. Two minutes. You're just not that smart. It's an hour or more to the hospital. We need to keep going."

The air turned icy. The streetlights made the wet streets and sidewalks swim beneath our feet. It was raining needles on our faces. He wiped his. I wiped mine. That was it. Tom Bender and me on the streets.

CHAPTER 40

THE COLD AND THE PAIN

An hour is an hour is an hour except in the rain. Then it's two hours.

"Either that hospital keeps moving," Tom said, "or we zigged so much we zagged ourselves lost."

I gave him a look. "Uh-huh. Or we don't want to get where we're going."

"Or all of the above. Plus, did you notice, the rain is turning. My father talked about snow. It'll be falling full blast in about...there. A flake. Another one. Is snow better or worse for us? It can snow above the freezing point, did you know that—"

"How can your brain keep bouncing around like this? Are you ADHD?"

"It's true. It's been known to snow as high as forty-nine deg—"

"You go from crying your eyes out—"

"I wasn't crying, that was rain on my face."

"—to joking dumb facts about science—"

"Science isn't dumb."

"I'm gonna scream!"

"Psychologists say—"

Someone yelled. A guy on the next corner waved his arms, I don't know at who or what. Something was going on. A car shooshed fast down the sloppy street. Then a quick rush of other cars, like a gang was chasing somebody. Downtown Bridgeport. Maybe this is what Mom meant. Everything was icy jagged black and the snow was coming wet and big and splattering the sidewalk. Gunning engines, then the cutting whoop-whoop of a police siren from a few blocks away. A van was suddenly racing, or maybe skidding, I turned and slipped off the sidewalk into the street, landing on my hand, while my cheek and ear smacked the curb and I screamed. The van veered away. Tom yanked me up by the arm I was trying to hold my head together with.

"Oww! My ear! Let me go!"

The sidewalk seemed all of a sudden pitched at a weird angle. I tried to palm snow onto my face with my scraped hand. Bloody water dripped down my neck. It felt like someone was jamming a chopstick into my head and my ear shrieked like a real herd of dragons. I tried to get my balance but fell to my knees and threw up instead. It was nothing but tomatoes, but must have looked like guts to Tom.

"Holy gross! Who did you eat?"

He tugged me to the end of the block and into a kind of alley between some apartment buildings where it was his turn to slip in the mush. He fell on his elbow and screamed and cursed. I laughed. "You too!" Cars screeched around corners. Bass thundered from sound systems. It felt like we were in a war zone. I threw open the lid of a giant trash bin to make a kind of tent behind the bin, and pulled Tom under it, tripping over my own feet and accidentally stepping on his hurt arm.

He groaned. "Oww! You idiot—"

"You are."

We huddled under the open lid of the trash bin, waiting for the pop-pop of gunshots, which I was certain would come. They didn't. Just an engine revving and, oddly, people laughing. We stayed put until the cars quieted and the loud bass drifted away and it was only the two of us. Nothing happened. Just people, moving around. Downtown life. My ear was a grinding ache now. I was tired and too frozen to move.

The alley that Tom had found was narrow, unlit, and night fell around us darker than ever, with white flakes dropping wet and fast onto the black pavement. By now his phone was dead. We didn't know the time. My head was a burning lump.

Somehow, under that funky metal tent, pain rolling through me, my legs and arms went limp and I drifted off. Not sleep, but exhaustion. I'd been moving every second since I woke up, hiding like an idiot at school, the trek to the hotel, Mom slipping on the stairs, my smelly house, this. The heaviness finally fell over me like a lead blanket.

I guess the two of us under there were warm enough, because in my dream I was inside. It lasted, what, ten minutes, two hours? I only know I smelled soup and went looking for it in the same mall as the public toilets from my other dream, which was fairly gross but at least I knew the places not to go in. When I woke up, my mind was gray, blank, dull, heavy.

"Do you smell soup?" I said, feeling crusty blood on my cheek.

"Yeah," he grumbled. "Duck soup." He was holding his arm in a weird position and rubbing his elbow and now his shoulder. "So I guess you're not dead."

"Not so fast. Maybe I am. That would explain why everything's so dark."

"I found a tarp in the trash. I hung it."

"Like curtains."

"All the comforts of—"

"Don't. What time do you think it is?"

He looked at his wrist. "Tuesday."

Stretching as much as I could, I pushed the tarp aside and hobbled out from under our roof. The snow had stopped but it was frigid, and what had fallen had stuck to the pavement. Everything was white and clean. The white streets rutted with black ribbons, the black brick outlined in white. The air seemed bright because of it, and the lights on the main street reflected clearly off the snow. We stumbled our way together to the corner, turned, turned again, and saw it, the hospital, a big white hazy glow and nearer than we had thought.

"Come on," I said.

"Carry me?" he said.

"In your dreams."

"No, I was thinking for real."

I wobbled forward like an old man. "Just keep going!"

CHAPTER 41
IN THE WHITE WORLD

Walking in the white world, step after step, we were finally near enough to the hospital to see people out front. It beamed clean and warm like its own city on a hill.

"Final push," he said, hunching his shoulders. "Right, left, right—"

All at once, a car was honking its brains out on the street behind us. Tom jerked around to watch. The car started to skid. I pulled him off the sidewalk as it bounced to a stop at the curb. The window slid down and a head popped out.

"Tom! Tom!"

It was Rich Downing, his mouth hanging open, his ski hat half off his head.

Mrs. Downing tore out from behind the wheel. "— been out of my mind! The police are looking for you! Everyone's looking for you. Jeff?" She seemed half surprised, half angry. "What in the world are you doing here? What happened to your face?"

"I fell—"

"We were together," Tom said, turning to me, then back. "I'm sorry I left, Mrs. Downing. It was dumb. I went to Jeff's house, then we got scared, and it wasn't supposed to take this long, or be long at all. Then Jeff mashed up the side of his head. I think he looks better this way—"

"Get in, both of you," she said.

Rich scrambled around to open the back door for us and we slid in, stiff and achy and soaking.

"Tom, I'm calling your dad," Mrs. D said, tapping her phone. "Jeff, where's your mother?"

"There." I pointed out the window. "The hospital."

Rich gasped. "Holy crow! What happened?"

As he waited for me to speak, his face was open and bright and taking it all in and I think I saw Rich for the first time. I wanted to answer, but the words pushed up from my throat to my chest in a hot, wet lump. My face must have looked dumb because I felt it crack in half, as if it were made out of cheap plastic. I cried, sloppy blubbery sobs down my cheeks, and I cried about my mother and the drinking and the cold and everything.

Tom translated. "His mother broke her foot. Jeff thinks it might have been her foot—"

"Why didn't you go with her?" Rich asked me.

"She told me to run and I did. Because she was drinking."

I said this or thought I did or it was a mess of sounds no one understood. But whatever I said, Tom nodded. "Yeah, pretty much a disaster, huh? We're sorry."

"Okay, okay," Mrs. Downing said. "First things first. Tom, we're taking you home."

———

A half hour later, Tom's father was half running, half sliding down their snowy driveway to the car. He pulled us both into a big hug.

Tom moaned. "Ow. I slipped and banged my arm!"

"And I slipped and fell on my ear!" I said.

But the hug went on. "Come inside!" Mr. B said. "I called the police and told them you two had been together all night and that you were safe. Come in. Come in!"

———

Mr. Bender must have had some kind of talk with Tom while I sat in the kitchen and they poked around for first-aid stuff for my scraped cheek and cut ear, which bled some but had stopped and was barely anything. Mr. B didn't seem mad, only focused. He called the hospital; Mom was sleeping, so he said we'd go there, "first thing in the morning."

"Which is...only three and a half hours from now," said Tom, pointing to the kitchen clock. "We almost made it."

Mr. Bender grumbled like we were wise guys but said nothing.

Good thing I took the first shower. Tom took at least a half hour for his. His dad finally pounded on the bathroom door. "Hot water doesn't grow on trees, you know!"

"Actually, a typical tree breathes out hundreds of gallons of water each day," Tom called back. "It's the large surface area of the leaves—"

"Does he do this to you, too?" his dad asked me. I nodded. He rolled his eyes. "Get. Out. Now!"

"Yes, sir!"

I wandered into Tom's room while his father tossed a cot together for me, shaking the covers and smacking the pillow like you're supposed to.

When Tom finally appeared from the bathroom, he sank onto his bed and only mumbled a few words before he started breathing heavily.

That cot was the best bed I'd ever had. Sleep was a warm ocean all night long. I took my time waking up, letting sleep pull away slowly like an outgoing tide. It didn't last. I heard the phone jangle a couple of times and knew it was over. After a quiet breakfast of eggs and toast, we drove through the sun-white streets to the hospital.

CHAPTER 42
HOSPITAL

Tom and his father stayed out in the hall.

The nurse said it wasn't just a fractured foot that Mom had. When they brought her in, her blood pressure was very low and her blood alcohol was high, way over two times something, so they were keeping her for a couple of days.

That, and because she had no one at home to take care of her, or even a home.

She was better this morning, the nurse said, and her vital signs were nearly back to normal. She was "on meds now," but didn't say exactly what kind, not that I'd know what meds did what.

I stood frozen at the door, not going in. No one said anything to me, no one forced me. I could enter or not enter. I understood, or thought I did, that everything I did or didn't do, or said or didn't say, was suddenly important and different from Mom's choices. Some things were actually up to me. Maybe there wasn't any stopping much of what was going to happen to either of us, but what I did, what I chose, would mean something.

Mom was propped up on the bed when I finally went in. She was looking out the window at the sky. Her foot and ankle were in a cast. A plastic bag with her clothes folded into it sat on the single chair. Tubes dripped into a thing taped on her wrist.

She saw my reflection in the window and turned.

"Jeff."

There was nothing but us leaking and blubbering for a few minutes, like Tom and I did last night. She gently touched my ear and face and asked if I was all right. "Yeah," I said. Moving the clothes bag, I shifted the chair closer to the bed and sat and told her what had happened. How I met Tom at our empty house, our dumb journey, everything up until Rich's mother picked us up.

"No police." I snickered. "They couldn't catch us."

She sank into the pillow, closing her eyes as she did. Her eyelids were wrinkled and darker than I thought they would be or should be. Had I never really looked at them before? Maybe I hadn't. Maybe they get like that when things don't go the way you want them to.

When she didn't open her eyes for a minute, then another, I listened to the beep of her heart monitor and just looked at her face, trying to take it all in. Grandpa's last words came to me then. *It goes fast. And only in one direction.*

If that was true, where was *this* moment on my timeline? Could anyone tell me? Mom, do you know?

No answer, just beep...beep.

She must have gone to sleep because of the medication.

"Okay, Mom. I'll come back later. Maybe we can talk then." I got up, shaking.

"Don't go," she said quietly. She reached for me, and I sat back down.

"They've been to see me," she said. "The Department of Children and Families. We have a case number. We are an actual case now, Jeff. In the system. We held them off for a good long time, didn't we? DCF, the marshal, the town. Mr. Andrade. You know he came here last night. How did he know? But he came. With flowers!"

I swallowed back a thing in my throat and she shook her head once. "It's been a while coming, hasn't it? You know it has, Jeff. We both know I'm a lousy mom."

"You aren't!" I said. "Mommy, I love you, and it's going to be okay. It'll get better. It will. Bit by bit, it'll get better. The job. You. I'll be better, too. I promise. We're like seeds."

Her eyes were brimming as she nodded and tried to smile through her snuffling, and she finally did smile. "You're a good boy," she said. Then the tears that had been waiting rolled down her face and chin and neck and I tried to dry them with the edge of her pillow but couldn't.

"The best," I said.

"Pretty darn close."

They came to get her up and wheel her to the place where she'd have some tests. Everything takes so long in a hospital. She held my hand in hers until a nurse pushed her wheelchair away through some doors. She was scared. I was scared watching her go.

I love you, Mom.

Maybe I said that out loud, but I probably didn't have to.

CHAPTER 43
WHAT HURTS TOO MUCH

I went back to Tom's house and stayed a second night. The cot wasn't as comfortable. I didn't sleep, rolled around a lot, but I found I didn't care about that and I knew it was okay that I didn't care about everything. Caring hurts.

The next morning, Mom's discharge day, Mrs. Bender was back. She had driven home during the night. She turned from the sink and smiled when I came down, hugged me for a long time, said some stuff and asked some, and started listening before I answered. I liked that Tom's father never talked much unless it was to push things forward. Mrs. Bender said if they'd known what was going on, Mom and I could have had Thanksgiving with them, which I was surprised to hear was only six days ago. It seemed weeks.

I must have said something back to her, but I really don't remember what.

Tom was all about showers now, and if nobody yelled

at him, he took his time, so I ate breakfast with his mom. When he finally came down, I went back up to the room and packed up the little junk I'd brought with me. I was going somewhere, I just didn't know where yet. Mr. B must have come in then, because on the way down the stairs I heard them all talking softly in the kitchen. It seemed private so I sat on the bottom step and waited.

"I mean it," his mother was saying. "For a while anyway. It doesn't make sense otherwise. If someone needs something different, we'll get something. We can get whatever they need. He can go to school without worrying."

"I don't understand." That was Tom. "'If someone needs something different.' What?"

"Like this, Tom. An agreement," his father said. I heard paper rustling.

"A legal thing your father found online," she went on. "The Gardners did it with Kevin. His parents signed it. Jeff's mother might if she understood it wasn't forever."

"It might solve some problems," his father added. "Quite a few..."

Tom was quiet for a while, reading I guess, then stood up, then sat down again, or something that sounded like that.

"Are you saying there's a way he can stay with us? Isn't that a foster thing?"

My throat tightened.

"Not exactly," his father said. "It's us, people he knows, not a strange family. I mean, we're strange. But maybe not to him. So much." He was trying to be funny, like I remembered him being, to get Tom to laugh. I didn't hear if he did.

"What do you think?" his mother said softly. "Sharing that way."

"I think it would be great," Tom said. My chest fluttered when he said that. "It would be great but I don't know if he would do it. I was…I was pretty crappy to him. Last year. And…I mean…he knows that. We talked about it a little, but he doesn't talk much. It's still there. It's still a thing…."

I tried not to listen any more. It was private. When I heard Tom push his chair I hurried back upstairs, to be there when he came in.

His eyes were wet as he told me what they'd been talking about, but he couldn't find the right words. He said everything in such a clunky way, full of "I don't know exactly" and "sort of" and "well, I mean," that I thought maybe I hadn't understood what I'd overheard, after all. My throat, already choked up, wouldn't let anything through.

I finally mustered enough breath to say, "Is English really your first language?"

"Ack! Let them tell you!" He nudged me downstairs into the kitchen. His parents were still talking, low, to each other. "Tell him," Tom said. "What we said. The plan."

They told me. "Guardians," they said. They showed me the agreement. "It's an option sometimes," they said.

I'd live with them, they said. Not permanently. Just until...

Watching Tom's eyes and face go through a bunch of expressions, I wanted to laugh, but it came out as a sob. "You can't even afford it! An extra person to feed?"

"Oh, no," Mrs. Bender said. "That's nothing you have to think about, ever—"

"But Tom told me about your job and all," I said to his father.

Mr. Bender shook his head. "That's not an issue, Jeff. It never will be. You being here will be a good thing. Especially for Tom. He's, well, you know. Really needy."

"Hey!" Tom said. Then he cracked a face at me. "Besides, what's to afford? You can eat what I don't want."

"Tom—" his mother started.

"Except I'll lick everything before you even get it," I said.

"Boys..."

"You're so funny, go stand up on your TV."

"I'll stand on your head instead."

"Boys."

CHAPTER 44

THE END OF THE BEGINNING

Things moved pretty quickly after that.

Mr. and Mrs. Bender found an attorney who did a lot of stuff I never saw. The attorney had her own agreement that was a few pages long, but Mom didn't trust it or lawyers and wanted to use the simple one Tom's father had found online so she could write in all the information herself. The attorney was okay with that.

It's called a temporary guardianship agreement, and for a single page it says so much.

Through the phone company, the lawyer tracked down my father in Jacksonville. Both she and my mother talked to him. He sent something called an affidavit, which he downloaded from the Internet and signed: *James R. Hicks.* Paper dad.

He agreed to let me make the decision. I could live with him or with the Benders. It wasn't really a question.

The lawyer also arranged that Medicaid would pay

for rehab for my mom. That's medical care the government gives to people who have zero money. The lawyer talked with the school people, and it turned out that going to school while living in another town wasn't a crime because even though we tried to hide it we hadn't done it for more than three months. It was only four and a half weeks since we'd left our house. It seemed twenty times that long.

I was there with everyone around a big table in the lawyer's office the morning before Mom went into rehab. She'd been staying the last week at the shelter, in the single women's wing. I couldn't imagine how it made her feel to be back there without me.

A copy of the agreement was sitting at each place. Tom sat next to me. The document was simple. I read it a few times. It was practically nothing, but it meant everything:

I hereby grant temporary guardianship of _____, of whom I have legal custody, to _____.

I watched Mom read it from top to bottom, then over again, holding the paper down with both hands on the lawyer's table like it would blow away, then sliding her fingers away as if she wanted it to. The lawyer gave her an ink pen, after taking the cap off and sliding it on the other end. I saw all these little things happen.

My mother put the pen tip on the page and slowly filled in our names.

First *Jeffrey A. Hicks.* Then *Mr. Robert Bender and Mrs. Emily Bender.*

There was also a place to mark the beginning and ending dates that I would live with them. My mother froze over that, looked at me for a long time, then at the calendar the lawyer had brought over, staring at the blank squares as if she were trying to understand another language.

What would the end date be?

Did anyone know when we would be together again?

"Or, the next line," the lawyer said, glancing at all of us, one by one. "We can use that as well. It might be simpler."

Mom read the next line, and I followed her eyes, already knowing what it said.

For as long as necessary, beginning on _____.

"It's December fifth," said the lawyer.

It was my life in numbers and scratches of ink. Mom's, too. For however long a time, she wouldn't be my mother, she wouldn't act as one. It was a hole in her life with me. Someone else would take over. Maybe she felt this was the real prison sentence. She wasn't fit to be my mother right now. Forget about me—how did that make her feel?

Her pen hung in the air, quivering.

I came around the table and hugged her and kept my head on her shoulder until she gently wiggled away so she could scratch in today's date and the year.

For as long as necessary, beginning on <u>December 5</u>...
Below that, she signed, then printed her name slowly, smudging it accidentally on her palm. She licked off the ink, somewhere between laughing and crying at the silliness of it.

The attorney read the paper over, handing it to Mr. and Mrs. B, who read and signed it, then to a man with a blue bow tie who wrote stuff at the bottom and pressed a seal on it. They did the same with all the copies.

"Done?" Mom said.

The lawyer nodded, smiling at my mother and me. "Done." She reminded me a lot of the shelter lady. She was as professional. And as sad.

Mom kissed me, then looked around the table. "Thank you. Thank you all."

Mom went into the rehab clinic at three PM. Their sidewalk was shoveled clean and salted. It was a decent place, as good as Medicaid would pay for, and it wasn't bad. Lots better than the Sidespot. I smelled cafeteria food from the lobby, and it smelled better than at school, too. We hugged and cried for minutes. The lady there was kind to me, to all of us. She asked if I wanted hot chocolate. I said no. She was the head doctor. Everybody was kind. Everybody was nice.

CHAPTER 45
BROTHERS

On the first day I felt okay enough to go to school, I went looking for Hannah. I found her at her locker. She didn't go away, which she totally could have, but listened, her eyes welling up, while I poured it all out in a sloppy, soupy goop.

"I've been in a shelter. My mom drinks. She's in a program now. I'm living with a friend. I just want to—can I—I was such an idiot to you and I know you didn't mean to—or anything, I was such a jerk...."

She was looking at me so intently and not saying anything and I wondered if she'd ever guessed that I'd wanted to touch her face in the library that day.

"Look, Hannah," I said, "the point is can I—can I..." I nearly couldn't get it out. "Can I buy you lunch sometime?"

She swept her arms around my back and pulled us together and put her chin on my shoulder. I remembered the girl on the train hugging the boy whose aunt had died and how it wasn't for real. This was for real.

A long few seconds later, she was looking at me again.

"I was such a jerk to you," I said.

"What? No. I'm sorry. It's just, I talked to your friends."

"My friends?"

"Josh. And Colin. From class? They said something might be going on. That you weren't—that something wasn't right. You didn't eat. I'm so dense. I didn't mean, my gosh, I didn't mean to hurt you, I should have just told you"—she wiped her cheeks—"that whole Carly thing, it was so insulting—"

"No. Hey. It was nice. It took effort. And four dollars. You're so cool. To do that. To think that way."

"I didn't want to lie," she said. "I just didn't know how to do it."

"It's okay, really. I try not to lie so much anymore either."

"So much?"

"Yeah, sorry. But look. This time, this time I promise to eat the pudding—"

At that she cried into her hands and made a sound like a little muffled yelp. I won't tell you what sound I made, but when we finally calmed down, the hallway was empty and the bell had rung twice and I was telling her about Jano and Tad. And finally I told her about Tom.

Mom's cell phone rang a couple of times that night. I didn't recognize the number, so I didn't answer it. I couldn't talk to her friends, if she had any left. I couldn't form the words I'd have to say.

The next day, or the day after, the temperature went down, more snow came. The big flakes falling made me remember Rich, who I hadn't seen since the night he and his mother found us. I called him.

"Hey," I said. "Look. Part of what I wanted to say in the car that night was thanks. Thank you for, you know, everything. All the things you did. Everything."

"That's okay," he said. His voice was low.

"But I wasn't," I said. "I wasn't okay. I was an idiot to you. To everybody. Lots of times—"

"Nah."

That word. It meant something else now.

"So, anyway, maybe we can hang out sometime?" He didn't answer right away. "If your mom says okay, I mean." I waited. "Or not, if she doesn't. You know, whatever." I was ready to hang up.

Then he said, "Sure. Cool."

We left it open.

———

The next day a voice mail from my father showed up on the phone. He wanted to know how Mom was, where she was, for how long, and so on. I waited a couple of days before I had the stomach to hear his voice.

"So, I'm with the Benders for a while," I said to him, pacing the backyard patio outside the kitchen window. It was three days after he called and late afternoon and dark and cold. "But I guess you know that."

"I'm sorry about this whole business," he said. "Life does that sometimes...gives you...never mind. It's good news, though. You used to be friends with the boy there."

"Tom. Yeah. We're friends." I looked up at the window of the room we were sharing now. "So, is that it? I mean, you called. You can't talk to Mom. You got me. I won't be able to visit her until next week, so that's kind of all the news, so..."

There was a pause. "Not quite," he said. I really wanted to hang up on him. "There's something you—a thing I need to tell you. It's about Erica."

"She dumped you, too?" I was channeling my mom now.

"No, no. Jeff, no. We're getting married. No date yet. But believe it or not, that's not really why I called. She—well, we—had our first ultrasound. You know what that is?"

I didn't answer. He thought I was so stupid.

"I guess you do," he said. "Well, it's all good,

everybody's healthy. We went back and forth about wanting to know, but she won. It's a boy."

"A boy," I said, wondering what I felt about it, if I felt anything. "Okay."

"A boy. Your brother. Jeff, you're going to have a brother."

My hands shook.

"His name is Jolyon. Jolyon Hicks, huh? That's what we've named him."

"Jolyon? Joe-lee-on. Jolyon. I guess that's cool."

"Yeah? You like it? Jeff and Jolyon. You have to come down."

Jeff and Jolyon. I thought of Jano and Tad.

"It'll be months, of course, but you have to meet him. And he has to meet you."

Jolyon Hicks. The name was bigger than he was. I liked it.

"Yeah," I said. "Okay. I don't know when. But yeah, okay, I will."

CHAPTER 46
THE HOUSE ON HARRISON STREET

A few afternoons later, I was in the backyard again, looking at the black trees. The backyard was my place, sepa-
rate from inside. Tom mostly respected that I needed a
space, and outside was it. Night was coming. It was frigid,
with the smell of mid-December snow inside the clouds.

Tom was doing something in our room. I didn't know
what until he came out and sat in one of the plastic chairs
on the edge of the patio stones, kicked his feet onto the
gray lawn, and gave out a breath that hung over his head
like a cloud.

"Jessica called," he said. "I told her what's going on,
what we've been up to."

I couldn't sit. I couldn't do anything but stand there.
"About me?"

"Yeah. She said good. That it was good. She meant it."

I nodded. "Tell me next time she calls, or you call her.
I should..."

"Sure." He looked up into the dark. "Gah. It's freezing out here! Don't you want a coat? I'm going inside. Here, take—"

"Don't start giving me stuff. More stuff."

The sound of the parkway was a high white noise behind everything. Crows, a few of them, came winging out of the night, black patches skimming the dark air. We tried to watch them, but the sky was already too black and deep to trace their flight.

"They stay," he said. "So many other birds get out of here in the winter. But these crows stay. They're called resident crows, did you know that?"

Inside, Tom's mother and father finished chopping vegetables and in my mind I heard a hiss from the stove as they dropped them into a pot of hot water. Mr. B was doing a lot more cooking since Mrs. B had found a job. I think he liked it. Sometimes he wore an apron.

"Speaking of money," Tom said, as usual, completely out of nowhere, "I told my parents I'll switch to public school, if they want. Plus, you can introduce me to this Hannah person."

"Never gonna happen."

I was actually planning to buy her lunch the next day. I saw her face in my mind and heard her voice, reciting the last chapter like she did in the library. I turned to him.

"What if I never find a place?"

His words were out before I could stop them. "You already have a—"

"Please don't tell me it's *here*. I'll kick you." His face was half in the shadow of the kitchen light. "We all know this is just a stop. Just a...bump."

"You can stay as long as you want."

"Your parents don't want that. *I* don't want it."

I was going to say something, repeat myself maybe, but my words caught in my throat. I didn't want to lie to him. I wouldn't stay here long and I couldn't. If I wasn't stuck here, then I was the opposite, a boat adrift, wondering where I might end up.

Tom could imagine next summer, four years from next summer, college, all that would come then, and this would still be home for him. I wasn't in any of those imaginings. Where would I be?

"It's good enough for now, right?" he said. "It's pretty cool, isn't it? Our room. The bunk beds?"

I didn't answer, looking off to the dark mesh of trees. A single white flake wandered down, then another, then a few.

"Your place will be wherever you are," he said finally.

I nearly snorted on him. "Does that even make sense?"

"I could probably figure a way that it would," he said.

"Don't strain your brain."

"Yeah, I should save it."

I won't tell you that Christmas came and the weather broke and the sun shone all January and Mr. Maroni gave me an A and Hannah became my girlfriend and Tom went back to being my sidekick and Mom was hired by the rehab clinic because she was so awesome. No. It actually snowed every other week through the end of February, totaling over three feet. There were nasty car accidents on the parkway because of it. One guy died on Christmas Day. Mom's problems didn't clear up right away either. It turns out you can't shake alcohol so easily. I never saw Hannah again after eighth grade, believe it or not, because Mom and I moved upstate where it was cheaper to live. Tom visited once and plans to again. Mom works at a walk-in emergency clinic now and once saved a little girl's life. It balances out.

But all that's another story, nowhere near its end.

And that night on the patio when those lazy snow-flakes fell? The night Tom and I were shivering out there together?

The whole sky opened and snow burst down heavy and thick and sudden.

We stood outside the house I belong but do not belong to and watched the flakes for a while, when a ladle or something clattered suddenly to the floor, and Tom's dad banged on the window with his palms, said something with a high laugh we didn't quite get, and Tom ran up the back steps.

"You coming?" he asked.

"In a bit," I said, and he went in.

———

I like snow. Now I do. I can choose to stay out in it or not. No one's forcing me to decide. It's up to me what I do. I make my own junk. The day I stood outside Mom's hospital room, choosing when to go in, I understood that. I understand it more each day.

Looking up into the heavily falling flakes I wondered if I would go anywhere. Be different enough from what I am now that I would be better. I didn't hate everything about myself, not really. I liked that I was quieter, which was new, maybe thinking a little more before I opened my mouth. That seemed a good start.

Tom tapped on the steamy window and made a face. "Jeff. Get in here!"

I went in. I did.

But in that split second when you're on the step between inside and out, half in the bright kitchen, half in the dark of the yard, it flashes through your mind how the cold can bite into your back, and icy flakes can sting your neck, and your fingers can tingle and stiffen on the door handle, and how it's warm and dry inside the house and it's pulling you into it, but you can linger as long as you want on the step, and if you go inside, you go inside because you decide to, you decide when and how to, and I chose to go in right then, at that moment, as clouds of steam surrounded me in room after room, every one of them smelling of soup.

AUTHOR'S NOTE

Some years ago I was in my town's public library and saw a boy at a table, leaning back in his chair and reading a book. He was alone, concentrating, as still as a statue. A common enough scene. It was after school and there might have been twenty or forty other students doing the same. What was particular about this boy, his expression, his attitude in the chair, I can't now recall, but in one of those strange moments that afflict (and bless) writers, I said, "That's Jeff Hicks."

The story of *Firegirl*, years old at that point, hadn't remotely been on my mind, but I suppose its characters Tom Bender and Jeff Hicks had never left the building. Whether this boy in the library stood up and returned the book to the shelf, or whether I later imagined he did, I no longer remember, but his reshelving of the book prompted a question: If he's engaged in it, which he clearly seems to be, why doesn't he just check it out? The answer came quickly: He can't bring it with him.

In that brief moment, *The Great Jeff* was born.

I want to thank my editor Alvina Ling for her brilliant

work here and in *Firegirl,* and for being open and even enthusiastic about a companion novel after more than a dozen years. I truly believe she loves these characters as much as I do. Many thanks also go to Nikki Garcia for her art in helping shape the narrative as an independent story with a heart all its own.

I am supremely grateful to Carla Miklos, executive director of Operation Hope of Fairfield (operationhopect. org), whose selfless and invaluable work in that agency provides housing and access to services for men, women, and families in unstable living situations. Her efforts to locate permanent accommodations to end the cycle of homelessness in my community create hope for all young people like Jeff. Carla's gracious generosity in discussing the center and in touring Operation Hope's facilities with me have made this a better book. The shelter appearing in these pages is not their shelter, and any inaccuracies and fictional liberties taken in describing it are, of course, mine alone.

I am thankful to Jeffrey McHugh for taking time out of his busy schedule as dean of students at Fairfield Woods Middle School to talk with me about homeless students and about the safety net of awareness and services in his school, services available to anyone confronting issues surrounding unstable housing. I have known Jeff McHugh, man and boy, for nearly six decades, and it's a great comfort knowing that an advocate of such sensitivity, eloquence, and grace has made the dignity and well-being of our young people his life's work.

My thanks must also go to Susan Costa, school counselor at Fairfield Woods, for describing the avenues of care offered to and provided for students in any kind of personal situation that affects their emotional health and happiness. Susan is another soul who helps maintain a system of response and aid with a single goal: the success of each student during his or her time in the school's care.

Conquering the fear and misplaced shame of using school or public aid services is something Jeff Hicks's mother, and indeed Jeff himself, battle with. Certainly every community is different, but even a brief look into the network of social services suggests that armies of good people are out there waiting to help our young people achieve the best life possible. Simply finding out about the many types of physical and emotional help available is the true first step.

My wife, Dolores, my daughters, Jane and Lucy, and my daughter-in-law, Sue, are inspirations every single day. Writing can often seem a detached activity, lonely and isolated, but having a loving family like mine is proof that the effort to create life on the page is a deeply emotional and spiritual business, wholly part of the continuum of family life.

A word about Mr. Maroni's book choices, his four short classics. *Out of the Dust* by Karen Hesse is as beautiful and heartbreaking and iconic as a photo by Walker Evans, and I have loved it for years. *Of Mice and Men*, well, John Steinbeck doesn't need my praise, but he has it. Stark and brutal, deep as a river, and slim as a dagger. *The House on Mango Street* by Sandra Cisneros is a poetic gem whose threads of language and whose moods and colors and vivacity come together in a perfect masterpiece, a touchstone for so much more than it is in this humble story. My hope, of course, is that readers will leap from here to *Mango* and devour it. *Pobby and Dingan* by Ben Rice. I bought this book years ago in a bookstore in Cape Cod mainly because it was short and I was completely shattered by its humanity and bright tragic humor, and by the fact that no one seems to know this brilliant miniature. This is Mr. Rice's first and only novel and I might be persuaded to trade every one of my hundred to have written it. I love this book, and I will keep telling readers about it.

Overall, I am deeply grateful to the many readers who have kept the characters of *Firegirl* alive for so many years. I hope this new installment will work its way into their hearts as well.

TURN THE PAGE FOR A PREVIEW OF

AVAILABLE NOW

Chapter 1

It wasn't much, really, the whole Jessica Feeney thing. If you look at it, nothing much happened. She was a girl who came into my class after the beginning of the year and was only there for a couple of weeks or so. Stuff did get a little crazy for a while, but it didn't last long, and I think it was mostly in my head anyway. Then she wasn't there anymore.

That was pretty much it.

I had a bunch of things going on then, and she was just one of them. There was the car and the class election and Courtney and Jeff. But there was Jessica, too. If I think about it now, I guess I would say that the Friday before she came was probably the last normal day for a while. As normal as things ever were with me and Jeff.

It was the last week of September. The weather had been warm all the way from the start of school. St. Catherine's has gray blazers, navy blue pants, white shirts, and blue ties, and it was hot in our uniforms. I sweat most of those days, right through my shirt, making what some of the kids called stink spots under the arms. We weren't allowed to take off our blazers in school, even when it was hot, so mine always got stained from the sweat.

Like most afternoons, I got off the bus at Jeff Hicks's house. We jumped from the top of the bus stairs and hit the front yard running, our blazers flying in our hands.

"You ever smell blood?" he asked, half turning to me.

Jeff had been my friend for about three years, since the summer after third grade. As we went up the side steps to his house, I remember thinking that he asked me off-the-wall questions a lot.

"What?" I said.

Jeff always said some strange thing, then waited, and I would ask "what?" so he could say it again and make a thing about it. He reached the door first.

"Did you ever smell blood?" he repeated.

"What does that mean?" I asked.

"Sometimes my mom comes home from the hospital all bloody from the emergency room —"

We rushed through the side door, making a lot of noise in the empty kitchen. Jeff's house was always unlocked, even though it had been empty all day.

"— some guy's guts on her shirt," he said. "It's so

gross. It's the coolest thing. So, did you ever smell blood?" He yanked open the refrigerator door.

"I don't know. Maybe. When I cut my finger —"

"That's not enough. I mean a lot. A whole glass of the stuff."

I felt my stomach jump a little. "A *glass* of blood?" I said. "Who has *glasses* of blood?"

He pulled out a tumbler of red liquid — blood? — from the refrigerator and began drinking. He drank and laughed and drank. I finally realized it was cranberry juice. The juice sloshed all down his chin and onto the front of his white shirt.

His shirt had little blots of red spreading down the front as he was dripping juice and laughing and watching me, until I laughed, too, at the whole thing.

"Stupid," I breathed. "How long did you have that glass waiting in there?"

Laughing even harder, he put the dripping glass on the kitchen table and wiped his mouth on his cuff. "By the way, I went for a ride in it last night." He went to the basement door and pulled it open.

I was still looking at the glass on the table. "Huh?"

He jumped down the stairs to a room with a TV and paneling. There were dark wooden shelves on the walls piled with stacks of his comic books.

I was right behind him. "You went for a ride in what?"

It was that game again. But I already knew.

"Duh. In your brain," he said. "My uncle's Cobra. I thought it was all you ever thought about."

"Yeah? The Cobra?"

He snickered as he went to the shelves. "The Cobra."

A Cobra is a classic sports car from the 1960s. I love Cobras. Not the skinny kind they made for a couple of years, but the fat one. You see them every once in a while. A Cobra is low and all curved and super-fat, like a chunky bug that's pumped up like a balloon. It isn't a family car. It's just two seats, a steering wheel, and pedals on the floor. It's a machine. The racing tires are really fat. The wheel wells over each tire flare out like big, angry lips. The front end of a Cobra looks like a snake, with two headlights like eyes and a big mouth (the radiator hole) that could suck the pavement right up into it. It's the nastiest-looking fast car on the road.

I love Cobras. I've built plastic models of them. I've bought magazines about them. I once went to an auto show with my father, and they had a red racing Cobra there. The shine was so thick it seemed like if you dipped your finger into it, it would be hot and wet. But they wouldn't let you get near enough to touch it. "As if it's so hot it'll burn you," I remember telling my father. He laughed. Cruise nights at a drive-in restaurant in the next town sometimes had a Cobra, too.

That past spring, Jeff had told me his uncle had an

original Cobra, and I was totally floored. He had restored it from a used one he bought in New York, where he lives. I had never seen the car, but Jeff told me it was a red one.

"The kind you like," he had said.

People don't really talk to me much in school or notice me, not even adults. My mother says it's because I don't "get out there." But Jeff and I had been friends for a long time. We never really said much to each other, but we did stuff almost every day. I always got his jokes, and I think he liked that. I remember feeling it was so cool that he knew I liked red Cobras.

Jeff had said his uncle sometimes brought it up to his house, and he got to ride in it. But I didn't get why I had never seen the car.

"I've never even seen your uncle," I said.

Jeff was flipping through a stack of comics he had taken down from a shelf. He chose one and slumped in a chair with it. He didn't say anything.

"I don't have an uncle," I went on. "I don't get the whole uncle thing. It's just me and my parents. Neither of them had sisters or brothers." He still didn't say anything, so I just kept on babbling. "Uncles always seem like these guys who get to have all the cool stuff fathers never get to have."

Finally, he dropped his comic into his lap and looked at me. "Yeah, well, my Uncle Chuck has a Cobra. And he's coming over next weekend."

I think my heart thumped really loudly. "Saturday? Next Saturday?"

He shook his head. "No, the weekend after. The ninth I think my mother said. Maybe we'll drive over to your house in the car." He pushed the comic book off his lap.

"Really?"

He got up. "My mom said she got me two *Avengers* and a *Spawn*, the one where he bites through to another world. But she hid them because I yelled at her. Let's find them. I need to get all the school junk out of my head."

"Really? You mean it about the car? The Cobra? You'll come over and we can ride around in it?"

"Sure. Let's check her bedroom."

Chapter 2

Monday morning, I slid into my seat in Mrs. Tracy's classroom.

It seems strange now to think that I didn't know anything about Jessica Feeney then. She was only a few minutes away, and I had no clue that she even existed. I had spent most of Sunday sitting on my bed with my car magazines around me. The window let all the warm air in, and I remember wondering if it would still be warm thirteen days later when the Cobra came.

My seat in class was the first one in the first row by the hall door. It was odd that I was even in the first seat. Where you sat in all the classrooms at St. Catherine's was alphabetical. In every year before, there were kids sitting in front of me. Bender isn't usually the first name. Kids with last names like Anderson or Arnold or Baker were some of the ones who sat in front of me in fourth, fifth, and sixth grade.

Two years ago, a girl named Jennifer Aaron sat at the head of the first row. She probably always had that seat, I thought. But I also thought it was strange because I had heard that Aaron was a Jewish name from the Bible, and why would a Jewish girl be going to a Catholic school? When I told my mother about her, she said I should just go ask her. But I never did find out. Jennifer transferred to public middle school last year, and two girls from the other class, Tricia Anderson and Cindy Bemioli, were in front of me for sixth.

Jeff hadn't been on the bus that morning, but he was already sitting in his seat next to me at the head of row two.

He didn't say anything when I said "Hey." He just sat there quietly and chewed his fingernails, which he did a lot, without thinking. I guessed his mother had driven him in because he missed the bus. She probably wasn't happy about it and so they probably had a fight. Jeff seemed to get mad a lot more since his father went away. Usually, I just left him alone, and pretty soon he'd be okay.

Right now his head was bent to the side, and he was turning his fingertips in his teeth. His tie was loose around his neck, and his top shirt button was undone. I remember thinking that his mother must have washed his shirt over the weekend, or it was an extra one because there were no spots on it. Maybe they had a fight about the shirt, too.

His legs dangled out into the teacher's area at the front of the classroom. Mrs. Tracy had asked him a couple of times already that year to reel his legs back in under his desk. He was stretching them out when she came in just then.

"Scoot your legs in, Jeff. Your slouching will curve your spine," she said. "You'll be a stooped-over old man by the time you're thirty."

She walked past and set down a pile of papers on the middle of her desk.

"Thirty *is* an old man!" said Jeff, taking his fingers out of his teeth and half looking around and laughing.

I snickered when I saw him joking. Maybe he was okay again.

Mrs. Tracy narrowed her eyes at him then smiled. "You'll feel different when you're that age. . . ."

"I know," he said. "I'll feel old!"

"All right, all right," she said, but the class cracked up anyway. Another busload of kids came in after the second bell rang. Melissa Mayer, who was sort of chubby like me, came in laughing with Stephanie Pastor, who looked a little like a boy if you saw her from the right side. Kayla Brown plopped a paper on the teacher's desk then sat behind me. She was freckled and had red hair and was as small as the girls in fifth grade.

Rich Downing came running in and jumped into his seat behind Kayla as if he was trying to win a race. His jacket was under his arm, and his shirt was coming out in the back. When he tucked it in I saw the same little V-shaped rip at the top of the rear seam of his waist that I had seen for the last couple of weeks. I knew that Rich was trying not to eat as much so his pants wouldn't tear on him, but it was happening anyway. The pants I was wearing that year were ones I had gotten last spring and that weren't too tight, so I wasn't in trouble yet. Like Jeff, Rich liked to crack jokes in class, but he was never as quick or as funny as Jeff.

Samantha Embriano came by and sat in the last seat of my row. She had black hair and a round face and eyebrows that almost met over her nose. She always said her last name together with her first name: Samantha Embriano. Samantha Embriano. It was always like that.

It would be like me calling myself Tom Bender. Hi, I'm Tom Bender. Tom Bender here. You just don't do that. I think at first she said her name like that because there must have been a year or two when she shared the same first name with someone else in her class. Samantha Baker or Samantha Taylor. But she continued to say Samantha Embriano even though that was not true anymore. Now we all called her that. Samantha Embriano.

Just after first prayers, when everybody stood up and held hands together and prayed along with Mrs. Tracy —

"Hold hands? No way," Eric LoBianco said every time —
I leaned over to Jeff.

"We're on for next weekend, right?" I asked. "Not
this one, but the next one?"

"Next weekend?" he said.

"The Cobra," I whispered.

Jeff's face unclouded. He smiled. "Yeah. My uncle's
coming over."

I smiled, too. Yeah, he's coming over and yeah, it's
going to be awesome. Mrs. Tracy was still fiddling with
something, and I scanned the room. I knew that no one
else in the class was going to be riding in an awesome red
Cobra next weekend. Or probably ever.

As I was thinking this and watching the last of the
bus kids get into their seats, my eyes finally came to the
last seat of the last row.

DISCUSSION GUIDE

1. Jeff and his mother seem embarrassed by their
    money and housing problems, and Jeff particularly
    goes to great lengths to hide these problems from
    his classmates, his teachers, and his friends—even as
    his situation very quickly gets worse. When you are
    in trouble, do you do the same as Jeff and try to keep
    your struggles secret from everyone else? If so, what
    things might you do to keep people from knowing
    the truth? If not, how would you go about letting
    people know? Who would you talk to first?

2. Jeff gets to know Hannah both in and out of school.
    Why do you think it takes him so long to tell her the
    truth about his situation?

3. At the beginning of the story, Jeff resents his old
    friend Tom Bender, certain that Tom told lies about
    Jeff and his mother. Do you think Jeff is being
    honest with himself about this? In *Firegirl*, Tom

concludes that it was Jeff who lied to him. The idea of telling the truth—or not telling it—is a theme in both novels. Do you tell lies? Why?

4. Jeff's eighth grade class is assigned several books to read and discuss: *Out of the Dust, Of Mice and Men, The House on Mango Street,* and *Pobby and Dingan.* Have you read any of these short novels? How do you think they might relate to what is happening in Jeff's life throughout *The Great Jeff*?

5. At several points in the story, the idea of *choice* is discussed by Hannah, when she talks about *The House on Mango Street,* and by Jeff, outside his mother's hospital room and again when he chooses whether to go inside or stay outside Tom's house. We often feel powerless to change our situations or our lives. Do you think you have the power to choose how you live your life and what happens to you along the way? What do you think *choice* means to Jeff?

6. By the end of *The Great Jeff,* Jeff and Tom appear to have resolved some of their differences. Is everything back to normal between them? What is and what isn't normal again? What parts of their relationship might be better than before?

7. Throughout the novel, Jeff says he is a funny guy even though people sometimes think his comments are mean. Jeff also states that because of his sense of humor, many of his classmates believe they can say "nasty" things around him. What does Jeff mean by this? What does this say about the power of our words?

8. In the last pages of the book, Jeff gives readers a glimpse of what happens to him in the future. Do you like knowing what is coming for him? How does your knowledge of what happens affect how you view his current situation with Tom?

READ MORE FROM
TONY ABBOTT

Edgar® Award winner

  LITTLE, BROWN AND COMPANY
BOOKS FOR YOUNG READERS

LBYR.com

BOB940

Thomas Sayers Ellis

TONY ABBOTT

is the author of over a hundred books for young readers, including the bestselling series The Secrets of Droon and The Copernicus Legacy and the novels *Firegirl*, *The Postcard*, *The Great Jeff*, *Lunch-Box Dream*, *The Summer of Owen Todd*, and *Denis Ever After*. Tony has worked in libraries, bookstores, and a publishing company, and has taught creative writing. He has two grown daughters and lives in Connecticut with his wife and two dogs.